A BOYISH GOD

Peter Alan Olsson

Strategic Book Publishing and Rights Co.

Copyright © 2013

All rights reserved – Peter Alan Olsson

No part of this book may be reproduced or transmitted in any form or by any means, graphic, electronic, or mechanical, including photocopying, recording, taping, or by any information storage retrieval system, without the permission, in writing, from the publisher.

Strategic Book Publishing and Rights Co.
12620 FM 1960, Suite A4-507
Houston, TX 77065
www.sbpra.com

ISBN: 978-1-62212-616-3

To Pam Olsson, MD, the love of my life. Pam's dedication to our profession and our patients is inspiring. Her psychiatric healing skills are peerless.

CONTENTS

Acknowledgments	vii
Foreword	ix
Chapter 1—A Boy Named Will	1
Chapter 2—Helpers	5
Chapter 3—On Evil's Doorstep: An Unsuccessful House Call	11
Chapter 4—Harry and Monica: Grandparental Love Defined	21
Chapter 5—So This Is Therapy?	27
Chapter 6—Evil's Shadows Appear	35
Chapter 7—Enter Jed Powers, Father God	41
Chapter 8—In Search of a Father's Love	45
Chapter 9—Will's Therapy Takes Hold	49
Chapter 10—Benevolent Authority as Therapy	55
Chapter 11—New Home Visits	65
Chapter 12—Satan Gets the Drop on Helpers	69
Chapter 13—Therapy Begins in Earnest	77
Chapter 14—No Easy Textbook Answers	83
Chapter 15—Enter Authentic Justice	87

Chapter 16—Son and Father	93
Chapter 17—Sacred Group Supervision	97
Chapter 18—Sacred Seven Gets Personal	105
Chapter 19—Ever More Sacred Seven	111
Chapter 20—Good-bye Jake Old Pal, et al.	117
Chapter 21—A Politically Incorrect Happy Ending	121
Postscript	127
Existential Addendum—A Dream of a Psychiatrist's Theology of Benevolent Revenge	129

ACKNOWLEDGMENTS

I am grateful to the following people, who have been helpful readers, cogent critics, encouragers, editors, and excellent consultants, in ways and domains too numerous to list. Pam Olsson, Bob White, Roger Hansen, Dan Blore, Larry Messner, Josh Messner, Dolores Messner, Nick Belsky, Susan Peery, Bob Kelly, Jules Bohnn, Marty Grothe , Janice Law, Don Jansen, Pat Barth, Linda Bilodeau, Gary Boeger, Nathaniel Olsson, Andrew Olsson, Meg Ivison, Shannon Guyer, Bill Moore, Jeff Houpt, Giles Lewis, Althea Horner, Ernie Hebert, Coleman Stokes, C.F. Kendall, and attorney Steve Waldman, who provided valuable information about relevant Texas law.

Finally, I thank all my teachers of psychotherapy, most especially the men, women, children, adolescents, families, and couples who trusted me enough to share their joys, sorrows, secrets, fears, and anxieties. My patients helped me listen better, as I helped them to help themselves.

FOREWORD

Novellas have many ways of being born. This one found its genesis when, after reading my book *Malignant Pied Pipers of Our Time*, my office janitor asked me, "Hey, Doc. If you treated Reverend Jim Jones when he was twelve years old, could the 918 deaths at Jonestown have been prevented?"

"Maybe," I replied.

Then this novella started unfolding. It is partly a memoir about my love of my work. The story is about the possibilities and profound difficulties in spotting false gods and changing destructive destinies. Unlike many melodramatic Hollywood movie scenarios, such changes occurring in psychotherapy are deceptively quiet and often muted. Psychotherapy involves many emotional experiences—anxiety, fear, fascination, wonder, boredom, humor and laughter, anger, sadness, and often pain. However, the more severe and ominous forms of pain, destruction, and even prevented deaths go unheralded. They are unnoticed because, existentially, they are like a suicide prevented—they never exist.

I hope that the character of Will Powers and his treatment can help thwart the evil of destructive cults by increasing awareness of the psychological dynamics behind the spawning of destructive leaders and their minions. In essence, be wary of all gurus!

The reader will recognize real places in Houston, but all characters in this novel are fictitious.

CHAPTER 1

A Boy Named Will

Will Powers's eyes can't be ignored. He is eager to "speechify," as he is fond of calling it. Powers stood behind a rickety podium and arched his four foot ten inch frame upward, stretching toward five feet through sheer force of will. His angry, walnut-colored eyes flashed as he ran his hand through his ebony hair during a cocky head toss. He summoned up what he calls his "fierce grin," then nodded at Jake in the front row.

Will once read that the Indians chose an animal for their spirit presence. He was certain his spirit presence was a raven—black, shiny, and scary, with a sharp beak that cuts and hurts. Jake, his best friend, was of a raven spirit, too. They were blood brothers. Will and Jake weren't afraid of anything when they were together. They would even kill if they had to.

Will's podium stood on a small stage at the far end of the old St. Thomas More School basketball gym, which served as a storage shed for athletic equipment, lawnmowers, a rarely used piano, and a jumble of folding chairs used only during the school's spring picnic. The old gym was hidden from view of the main campus by the overshadowing, new, chrome-and-glass gym and auditorium.

The stale smell of cigarette smoke lingered from the teachers and staff who sneaked breaks in the abandoned gym. The fall day in Houston was smothering, with an eighty-eight degree, high humidity, sweaty-armpit atmosphere. A dusty Troop 66 Boy Scout flag and a drooping Sunday school banner stood near the podium like two old soldiers from a forgotten parade. The flags made Will feel more important, powerful, and official.

Will came to enjoy the smoky, humid atmosphere around the podium when he frequently sneaked in after school. He liked to practice his future preaching and sermons. In a few years, Will knew he would preach at the Astrodome or Reliant Stadium. He imagined the old gym as a grand auditorium filled with riveted listeners soaked in sweat from the power of his words. He wasn't like that sweet, weak-voiced Joel Osteen of the Lakewood Church on TV. Will's sermon would transfix and enrapture his imagined flock. Will and Jake knew those Lakewood Church people sat like an audience of frightened sheep. Will's powerful words would rip through the fetid air and strike people's hearts. Someday he would preach to a thousand people. They would get scared of Satan's power. The power of Lord Will Powers, preacher king of Houston.

Will grasped the podium tightly, extended his head toward the ceiling, and jutted his chin forward and up as he prepared to speak. His jugular veins bulged like small, blue ropes under his flushed skin. He introduced himself to his imagined, rapt, and sweaty audience, and then winked at Jake in the front row. Will's voice was deep and affected. His dark eyes flashed. He felt so alive his skin tingled. It felt like electricity shooting up his spine to spark his words. He gripped the lectern with white knuckles. If he was prevented from preaching, he would have to kill someone!

"My name is William I. Powers. The 'I' in the middle means Isaac, some guy in the Bible's Old Testament. I never tell anyone about that name, because I hate it. I guess my mother thought it sounded important, but it sounds stupid, like my mother. I want to say important things to you right now. I'm twelve years old, but you'd better listen to me or I can hurt you. Kids don't get to talk much, especially at St. Thomas More School. Adults don't listen to kids much anyway, at any time or anywhere, especially when we say stuff that bothers them. Then they start telling, not teaching or listening. Grown-ups always feel they have to be in charge. They like to tell kids what to do. Grown-ups are stupid. Hey! You in the back row! Quiet! Now! I go to this school, but I hate it. It's a Catholic school, and most of the teachers are nuns and priests. They really like to boss kids around, because they don't have kids of their own. I don't think they even have sex. I could be a good priest. I could be a better teacher than any of those nuns and priests at my school. Most of all, I'd tell the truth about death and being dead. We people are just animals. When we're dead, we're gone into dirt. There is no heaven or hell. My dad and I spend a lot of time at libraries and reading books. He and his men friends in the Last Saturday Night Club are the only grown-ups I like. They're the only smart men I know. My dad is their leader. My dad says that if they can find a smart woman, she can be a part of the club. Maybe I won't hate you if you're smart and listen to me—I mean really listen! I think listening is real hard to learn, because no grown-ups do it very well. They're too busy thinking up the next thing they'll tell us. Right, Jake?"

Jake nodded and grinned in the front row. A door creaked open at the far end of the gym. Will scooted out the back door and jumped on his bike.

CHAPTER 2

Helpers

Dr. Tom Tolman's office phone buzzed. Yanked from his reverie on the doorstep of a nap, he unhappily remembered that he agreed to cover the phone for his secretary during her lunch break. A nap would have been nice. Answering the phone robotically, Tom heard the voice of Sister Andrea Albright from St. Thomas More School.

Sister Andrea had Tom's vote for sainthood. They worked together on community mental health projects in both her parish and the Houston community for many years. They wrote articles together on destructive, exploitive cults. She referred many good patients to him, which meant people who really wanted help. They were willing to look at their own responsibility to change their attitudes and behavior. More importantly, they were responsible about paying their bills.

Sister Andrea jokingly called those things "Tolman's Laws of Good Patienthood." When a patient couldn't afford his services but really needed therapy, Sister Andrea found church funds to help pay for it. She didn't want Tom writing prescriptions for drugs to answer a patient's problem, and he liked that. She was pretty and a good, perceptive soul.

"Sister Andrea, how's business?" he asked.

"Tom, I'm concerned about a twelve-year-old boy," she replied. "I hope you'll agree to give him psychotherapy. He has superior intelligence, talent, and unusual charisma. His anger is palpable, and he seems obsessed with *death*."

"Andrea, this is a bad day. After the attacks on the World Trade Center and the Pentagon yesterday, I'm blown away. I just learned my ex-wife Joan died at the World Trade Center. I've been seriously considering retirement for the first time in my professional life."

"I'm sorry to hear about Joan," said Sister Andrea, "but you can't retire yet. I won't let God let you. After 9/11, we need you even more. This boy needs you more than most. Let's meet, so I can tell you more about him."

"Okay, I'll talk. Your place or mine?"

"Mine, so you must behave yourself."

They agreed to meet at six o'clock the following day.

* * * * * *

The front of St. Thomas More Church was an expanse of stained glass with a scene of dozens of children surrounding the kindly image of the storytelling savior. Jesus held the children in rapt attention, and their faces shone with smiles.

Tom enjoyed seeing the church. Attractive shrubs and multicolored flowerbeds graced the entryway to the sanctuary, which faced the main street. The rear of the building was plain brick. Beyond the parking lot were playgrounds, the new gym, and baseball and soccer fields. A grassy field formed the front yard for the chancery of the Catholic diocese. Late-afternoon sun reflected gold off the windows. Sister Andrea's office was in a private corner of the chancery.

Tom relaxed in Sister Andrea's simple waiting room. The chairs and sofa were comfortable, and the magazines were up to date. *Time, The New Yorker, The Economist,* and *The New York Times Book Review* provided depth beyond *Reader's Digest,* and there were several Catholic magazines, including *Faith & Family, Catholic Forester,* and *US Catholic.*

Sister Andrea's office door burst open, and an eleven- or twelve-year-old boy flashed a tight smile as he walked quickly past Tom and out of the waiting room. He moved gracefully, like a cat, and had piercing, dark eyes and jet-black hair. Tom glanced out the window and saw the boy speed off on a battered, old bicycle. Sister Andrea appeared at her door with a fretful expression.

"Come in, Tom. That was Will Powers who breezed past you. I hoped to introduce him to you, but he said, 'Not today and maybe never.' "

Tom settled into one of Sister Andrea's comfortable chairs. Even wearing a habit, she was an attractive woman. On occasions when she was serious, concerned, and creatively engaging a clinical problem, she looked particularly beautiful.

What a waste, he thought. *She'll never experience the tangible, erotic, special love of a man.*

She broke his reverie.

"As you know, Tom, I've seen many troubled and depressed kids.

I rarely overreact. I'm the opposite of hysterical. This one, though, really troubles me. I'm afraid for him. For a twelve year old, Will has intelligence and unique gifts of charisma and leadership, but he also has the potential to be cruel, hurtful, and even evil."

Tom said, "There's nothing wrong with charisma, Andrea. Will certainly has an intense smile. Actually, it's appealing."

"One of the nuns found Will conducting a funeral for a dead bird in the corner of the schoolyard during recess. Ten spellbound kids sat around as Will preached and buried the bird."

"Some people would see that as cute, even touching," said Tom.

Sister Andrea pressed further.

"Sister Mary Agnes quietly observed the funeral at first. Then Will's sermon took on a loud, angry, hateful tone. He told the kids they'd die someday like the bird, and their parents couldn't protect them. Will said they would turn to dirt when they died. He smiled when several kids cried. A spunky eleven-year-old girl, Penny Paulsen, told Will to stop being hateful and evil. Will jabbed Penny in the face with a pencil. He almost punctured her eye. It bled. When Sister Mary Agnes interrupted the proceeding, Will jabbed at her with the pencil and kicked her, saying he was better at funerals than any priest. He gave Agnes a nasty look before walking off. Agnes took Penny to the nurse's office. She said most of the younger kids were frightened of him except gutsy Penny Paulsen, yet, many kids still follow him around at recess periods. Like Will has some power over them."

Tom asked, "Have you talked to Will?"

"I've spent several hours with him. Will claimed Sister Mary Agnes was menacing him. Tom, he has read an incredible amount about theology, philosophy, and spiritualism. His favorite topics are death, life after death, and socialism. He talks a lot about what he calls socialist heaven. Will says Satanists, animals, and Communists might make it there, but never Catholics, Protestants, or Jews. If I merely listen, he rambles on and on. If I interrupt, he becomes irritated and arrogant. When I confronted him about the incident Sister Mary Agnes observed, he told me to go drink communion wine and abruptly left my office. I've tried calling his parents, but apparently no one's home during the day or early evening. Tom, I'm worried about him. Will you take his case?"

How could he turn Andrea down? But Tom sensed the therapy would be one of those *challenging ones,* but he always had strong rescue fantasies about needy kids. Besides, he liked and admired Sister Andrea.

"You know I can't turn down one of my best referral sources," he said, "even if I plan to retire soon. Let's discuss the parameters and boundaries of treatment, and I'll get started, assuming he'll see me."

Tom learned the hard way over the years that a case like Will's required special planning and anticipation of trouble in the boundaries of treatment. At the age of twelve, Will wasn't a true adolescent or a typical child-therapy case.

After a lengthy discussion, Tom and Sister Andrea agreed that he would schedule two therapy hours for Will each week. The sessions would occur in her office, where Tom occasionally saw consultations regarding children or their parents at St. Thomas More. When family or couples sessions could be arranged, Sister Andrea took over duties.

Sister Andrea learned that half of Will's tuition was paid by his maternal grandparents, Harry and Monica Marshall. The other half came from the scholarship fund of St. Thomas More Church. Will's parents, Jed and Mary Powers, had agreed to participate in Saturday cleanup activities at the church kitchen as their contribution to the school, but their attendance remained at the bare minimum.

Will's maternal grandparents were retired but remained faithful members and contributors to St. Thomas More Church. Will's parents weren't members. As usual with patients paid for by the church, Tom would be paid $75 per hour instead of his usual $150. The treatment plan would be summarized in a letter to Will's parents.

A preliminary letter from Tom and Andrea was sent to Jed and Mary Powers to schedule a meeting with them, wherein they would discuss the situation and their treatment recommendations for Will.

CHAPTER 3

On Evil's Doorstep: An Unsuccessful House Call

Tom could have predicted it. Sister Andrea called to say Will's parents hadn't responded to the letter or her repeated phone calls. They decided to send another letter announcing their visit to the Powers home at ten o'clock the following Saturday morning to discuss Will's situation. Tom usually enjoyed the rare home visits he made, because they triggered his fantasy of being an old-fashioned country doctor.

Late September and early October in Houston can be delightful for a few precious days or weeks. That Saturday was one of those glorious days. The temperature was cool, and the clear blue sky and gentle breeze brought to mind football games and long walks.

Tom met Sister Andrea at Jerry's Donut Shop, midway between his Meyerland-area office and her church campus office. The Powers home was within comfortable walking distance of both offices. As usual, Tom arrived early. He thought about his dead ex-wife Joan, who always loved this kind of day. After their divorce, Joan quickly moved back to South Bend, Indiana, where the more-frequent cool weather pleased her.

Tom and Joan had met at Notre Dame, and their first date was on a cool, clear, fall evening. He always thought about Joan on days like that and felt an abrupt jolt of pain over her recent death at the World Trade Center. His discovery of her affair sixteen years earlier and the memory of their divorce no longer stung as much.

Recently, he became aware of how his own affair with psychiatry and psychotherapy fed into the complex web of factors leading to their divorce. Tom mused that divorces have as many causes as marriages.

Sister Andrea tapped his shoulder.

"Hey, Doc, a penny for your thoughts."

"Oh. Hi, Andrea," said Tom. "You know us shrinks and our free-association thing."

"Most people call it daydreaming."

Knowing nothing about Mr. and Mrs. Powers, they sensed the visit might be difficult. After the short walk, they stood on the brick steps of a plain, brick-veneer, two-story house. The window curtains were drab gray. There were no flowerbeds or window boxes. Tom noticed a peculiar, turret-shaped brick structure adjoining the garage at the end of a glassed-in breezeway connecting the house and garage. It resembled a small castle. The only windows in the odd structure were near the top. It appeared to have a door into the garage and breezeway.

Tom pressed the doorbell. After several rings, a man opened the door wearing a plain white T-shirt and wrinkled khaki pants. Scuffed slippers covered his feet. His face was flushed red, and his belly protruded over his belt.

Jed Powers had a mild wheeze, and they caught the faint odor of beer on his breath. He stared at them with peculiar bloodshot eyes that were large, watery, and dark blue, and seemed remote and angry. Tom was reminded of a hooked walleye.

"What do you two want?" Powers asked.

"I'm Dr. Tolman, and this is Sister Andrea Albright. We're from St. Thomas More School. Are you Mr. Powers?"

Jed seemed disinclined to talk, but he replied, "Yeah, I'm Jed Powers. What do you want?"

Tolman ventured, "I hope you received our letter about this visit. We tried to call several times. It's important that we talk to you and Mrs. Powers about your son, Will."

"Is he in some kind of trouble? Is he flunkin'?" He didn't invite them inside.

"Will's grades are good, Mr. Powers," Sister Andrea said, "but we need to discuss some things about his behavior with you. May we come in?"

Jed growled, "No. My wife's asleep."

Andrea took out her appointment book, saying, "May we make an appointment for early next week? Morning, or evening?"

"I'll talk to my wife and have her call you," said Powers.

Before they could say more, he closed the door. As they turned to walk back toward the street, Tom glanced up at a second-floor window and saw Will peering out. Tom waved, and Will flashed that quick, tight smile that was filled with anger yet slight warmth. From within the house came the muffled sounds of an angry conversation.

Tom invited Sister Andrea to lunch. Because she had no commitments until the evening, they had time for a lengthy discussion about Will and his family.

Sister Andrea said, "Mr. Powers didn't even know that Will's grades at school are good."

They discussed Jed's shoddy appearance, beer breath at ten-thirty on a Saturday morning, and anger, and then tried to decide on a further treatment plan. If the Powers didn't call back by midweek, they agreed to request a meeting with Will's grandparents, Mr. and Mrs. Marshall. In the meantime, Andrea would keep in touch with Will at school.

Abruptly, she said, "Tom, I'd like to offer a prayer now."

After a thought about how authentically angelic, kind, and beautiful she looked, he said, "Of course, Andrea."

She bowed her head, praying, "Father, we face something very powerful, perhaps evil, in the family atmosphere of Will Powers. We can't ignore our intuitions. Help us have the strength and grace to proceed with our efforts to help Will. The destiny of this boy is in your able hands. As we proceed in our efforts to help, we value your active presence. In Jesus's name, amen."

They sat in silence. Tom was fascinated by her request for God's active presence. The silence was peaceful. He dealt comfortably with silence during his therapy sessions with patients, but often with friends, and particularly girlfriends, long silences felt awkward. He promised himself to write a paper someday about the many forms of silence; it reminded him of how the Eskimos had many terms for different forms of snow. At public meetings, when someone requested a moment of silence, Tom looked around impatiently and often squirmed.

Tom said, "Andrea, we've known each other a long time. I often wanted to ask why you entered the order. Do you regret not marrying and having children?"

"I don't often answer those questions," said Sister Andrea, "but because I trust and respect you, perhaps you'll understand when I say that I *am* married and have children."

Of course, he thought, *she's symbolically married to Christ and His church. Her children are the kids in the parish, and they're fortunate to have her to love and care for them.* He blushed, saying, "Sorry. I forgot my practical theology for a second. Andrea, part of the reason for my question stems from how much I respect and admire you. I've been divorced for ten years, and though I've dated several women, seldom do they have the depth of feeling for life that you do. You're probably my best woman friend. Several women I've become close to since the divorce have broken up with me, saying I'm too serious. I'm no fun, married to my work, and too much into my own head."

Andrea smiled with shyness and with wryness. She said, "Dr. Tolman, you flatter and embarrass me. If I didn't know how sincere and serious you are, I'd think you were flirting with me." She giggled softly. "By the way, have you ever thought of being a priest?"

Tom blushed a bit more, saying, "Sister Andrea, now we're both embarrassed. My mother probably wanted me to be a priest. She disliked my profession, saying it was strange. My dad called psychiatry, 'The analysis of the id by the odd.' A compromise with my parents kept me out of seminary, but anger at my father drove me to Notre Dame, where I received a partial scholarship. I did jobs on campus to pay for it. My father offered no financial help, saying the priesthood or Protestant ministry offered me a free education and a lifelong meal ticket. His attitude helped lead me into psychiatry. Psychiatrists are adulterated clergy, anyway. Jed Powers reminds me of my anger at my father. It's a horrible feeling to be discounted or told who or how to be."

There was a long pause. Finally Andrea said, "I sense something very wrong in that home, it goes beyond the apparent psychological neglect of Will by his parents. Whatever Mr. Powers's psychological problem is, he's an agent of something more evil. I know it, smell it, and sense it. It was jarring when he shut the door in our faces. I'm sure you heard the angry voices inside the house as we walked away. I saw Will peer out an upstairs window. Looks like we're back to square one of epistle writing."

A serious, feisty, attractive look came to her face.

"If we don't hear from Mrs. Powers by next Wednesday, I'll schedule a meeting with his grandparents. They'll probably see us and might help. I have to return to my office for paperwork before a parish social function this evening. Why don't you come to supper at the parish hall at seven?"

Tom begged off, quipping, "Sister Andrea, tomorrow is my once-a-month token church door darkening. I have a pact with myself never to do it more than once a month."

He enjoyed her playful departing scowl and drifted into his inner thoughts. It was difficult for men to feel friendly, trusting, and close to women. The alpha male sexual conquest thing often intruded. It took the safety net of her being a nun to allow him to value her as a respected colleague and friend. He found her physically attractive.

Her kindness, dedication, and love of life led him to value her as a special friend.

Friendship is a rare, precious presence in anyone's life, including his. As he left the restaurant, he thought about her genuine fear for and concern about the Powers family. Though he hadn't felt the same degree of fear she expressed, he had to respect not only her clinical judgment but her spiritual intuition.

Then came a sudden wonderful thought, like an inner joyful shout: *By God, I love her!* No denial or intellectualization was allowed, nor did he need to apologize to anyone. He simply loved her. His realization was clear, vivid, and thrilling.

* * * * * *

Sister Andrea loved walking, especially in the cherished, cool fall days that occasionally graced Houston. The streets near St. Thomas More were lovely. Elegant, old oaks lined the streets, and children played in front yards.

Her thoughts were jumbled. Tom Tolman was a uniquely tender and loving man. Despite the traces of machismo he occasionally displayed, he always impressed her. She liked him. If she'd ever had a brother, she would have wanted one like him. At forty, Andrea could imagine herself married for twenty years to a special man like Tom. His psychiatric skills and awareness might have allowed him not to think of her as weird. Many young men had during the awkward, hormone-saturated years of her late teens. Back then, she sadly interpreted her spiritual gifts as a problem.

Her dad often kidded her for being absentminded; she was sometimes so wrapped up in reading the Bible that he had to shake her to get her attention. She never told her parents about her occasional intense, accurate intuitions of things that were about to unfold. She often felt a strong sense of emotional connection to everyone and everything around her. She felt the spirit aura near a beautiful piece of art or a well-written poem. The sensation grew painful, however, when there was a bad or evil person nearby. One psychologist, during her clinical social work training, joked that she could detect a psychopath or criminal on the basis of her sixth sense. She felt that about Jed Powers.

Friends shook their heads or teased her when she looked for a long time at a simple thing like a flower and talked about how wonderful it was. Even her dad frowned when she discussed her belief in miracles. It once bothered her that so many people didn't recognize a miracle when it occurred in front of them or actually happened to them. She often chuckled with the everyday

angels in charge of the effort to express God's grace. Years later, she asked herself another question: Why were so many men such psychological and spiritual midgets? If a young woman was tuned into spiritual and intuitive issues, why were so many young men insecure about such talent? Why did they call it weird or shun her?

After many years, Andrea concluded that most men were raised in an insecure, ignorant climate when it came to spirituality and spiritual awareness. In recent decades, liberated men who were in touch with their feelings had reached a higher percentage in American society. Only perhaps 20 percent of American men had emotional IQs over one hundred. Tom's must be well over 130, and his spiritual IQ about 115, but she knew she could improve that. The thought made her giggle.

During her teen years, only 2 percent of men had EQs over 100. Spiritual awareness in modern men was still at 1 percent. Andrea valued, accepted, and cherished her spiritual gifts. She enjoyed moments when she had feelings of great joy. Offering no apologies to anyone for those feelings, she felt proud of her spiritual maturity.

She also really liked Tom Tolman a lot. Thinking of his smile, she giggled again.

CHAPTER 4

Harry and Monica: Grandparental Love Defined

When Wednesday came without any phone call from the Powers, Sister Andrea quickly made an appointment for her and Tom to meet with Monica and Harry Marshall, Will's maternal grandparents.

Sister Andrea and Tom met briefly in her office before the Marshalls arrived. As he saw the older couple through the office window walking to the entrance of the waiting room, Tom was touched. They held hands. Sister Andrea noticed the affection, too, and smiled.

The Marshalls were in their late seventies. Harry was six feet tall with broad shoulders. His leathery skin had seen many days outdoors in the hot, humid Houston summers. He had a warm smile, but his shoulders were stooped and his skin was pale. The smile lines and wrinkles on Monica's face were her dominant pattern except when the conversation turned to her grandson, Will. Then her smile glowed.

Monica was pretty, and her gleaming gray hair was kept in a

simple, elegant ponytail. For decades, she volunteered at the school's library. Sister Andrea heard often of how the children and parents loved Monica.

They briefly discussed their mutual fondness for St. Thomas More and the school. Then Sister Andrea began probing about Will by describing his behavior at the school. She gently expressed concern about the boy.

Tears filled Monica's eyes. "We rarely see Will," she said. "For many years, Jed, who dominates our daughter, has allowed us to visit only on major holidays. He never lets Will visit or play at our house after school anymore. Mary occasionally calls or stops by briefly, but her demeanor has changed. She used to be lively and fun. In recent years, she's become passive, and her emotions seem frozen. It's as if she's looking over her shoulder to see if Jed's watching."

"Mrs. Marshall," Tom asked, "have you witnessed any physical abuse of Will or Mary by Jed?"

"No, Doctor, but I sense Jed intimidates Mary psychologically. There are never any physical bruises, but between the lines of her conversation I hear her fear of Jed. At first in their marriage, things were different. They took Will to the park or the zoo. They saw movies, and we babysat Will. For the last six or seven years, Jed has grown progressively colder, distant, and hostile toward my husband and me. I think he hates the church. You know we pay for part of Will's education. Jed would never do that. Doctor, I'm not usually a worrier, but I've become one lately. Jed's eyes have grown cloudy, filmy, and sometimes dark. He won't look people in the eye. What worries me is that there's a strange bond between Jed and Will.

There are no smiles, laughter, or fun times between them, but, according to Mary, they apparently spend a lot of time reading together in Jed's study and visiting the library."

"Doctor," Harry said, "in recent years I've become frightened of Jed. In my fifty years in the construction business, I knew some violent, mean, and strange men, so I don't scare easily. When Jed and Mary first married, it seemed I was becoming close friends with Jed. We had coffee or took long walks together a couple times a month, and we played golf occasionally. Jed once told me he was close to his mother, Jane, but then he described his father as cold, cruel, and rigid. Val and Jane Powers died when Jed was in his early twenties, so Monica and I never met them. Val was a construction worker and a Pentecostal minister. He promised Jed he was saving money for Jed's college tuition. Jed wanted to become a veterinarian. Suddenly, Val insisted that the money would be used only if Jed attended seminary. Jed, feeling bitter, left home and tried to work his way through pre-vet school. Mary met him at the University of Houston, where she studied elementary education. Jed quit college after two years, because he made good money taking care of the dogs and other animals used for research and training by medical students and doctors at Baylor College of Medicine. He said his and Mary's salaries would allow them to have a family, but only one child.

"The frightening things about Jed began seven years ago," he continued. "There was a special Saturday evening program at the parish hall at St. Tom's. We got a babysitter for Will, and the four of us went to the supper and heard a guest speaker, a priest from San Francisco who was an expert on Satanism and exorcism. Many parents were interested, because they had heard reports of teenagers' involvement with Satanism. It was a spooky evening. The priest read several scary passages from *The Satanic Bible* and Anton LaVey's writings. Jed was enthralled. He took references and notes during the talk and was quiet on the drive home. That's when it began. Since then, Jed has become increasingly distant, and so has Will. Jed used to attend mass with us occasionally, but he always seemed bored or angry. Now he never goes to church. Will won't even go to Sunday school anymore. If our daughter didn't stand her ground about Will's school, I'm sure Jed would have the boy in public school. Mary attended St. Tom's and adored her teachers and the program. Monica and I still gladly pay part of Will's tuition."

"Mr. Marshall," Tom asked, "have you tried to talk to Jed about your concerns?"

Harry looked very sad, saying, "When I tried to talk to him, his expression was a mixture of a smirk, sneer, and threat. He told me my church was a pitiful, boring den of hypocrites. Then he walked away. I didn't press him further. What can we do, Doctor?"

Tom explained that he and Sister Andrea had already discussed Will's family situation in detail. They proposed an unusual approach that would require the Marshalls' signature and agreement.

He handed the Marshalls a copy of a lengthy therapy contract for them to sign. In essence it asked, because they were paying for part of Will's school tuition at St. Thomas, and Will's parents hadn't responded to the school's repeated requests for a meeting, that they give their permission for Tom to see Will for therapy sessions every week on Tuesday and Thursdays. Sister Andrea would continue to offer monthly family or couples sessions to the Powerses via registered letters. Dr. Tolman and Sister Andrea would discuss Will and his family's treatment with their peer-supervision group. This group discussion would be completely confidential.

Sister Andrea and Dr. Tolman would meet with the Marshalls every six weeks to report on the progress of Will's treatment. Looking worried, the Marshalls signed readily.

Tom and Sister Andrea had already discussed their treatment plan with the priest and principal of the school. Sister Mary Agnes, the headmistress, said Will could continue at the school only if such treatment was undertaken.

Tom and Sister Andrea remained worried about the situation. They discussed the Powers family in detail at their monthly Sacred Seven peer-supervision group, where one member said, "That family will be a major challenge."

Tom and Sister Andrea's Sacred Seven peer-supervision group, support, and collaboration would be crucial for treatment success with the Powers family.

* * * * * * *

Mary Powers called Sister Andrea for an appointment, which was promptly made. When they met, Mary had a tight frown and spoke softly.

"Thank you for seeing me, Sister. I'm afraid. I don't know where to turn. Seven years ago, I noticed my husband, Jed, and our son, Will, gradually and relentlessly changing. They morphed into a state of detachment and emotional coldness. We used to go to the zoo, the planetarium, art museums, and movies on weekends. We enjoyed life as a family. We laughed and played board games. God, how I miss the laughter. When Jed and I first met, I was studying at the University of Houston. We didn't have much money, but we had fun. When Will started school at St. Thomas More, we pitched in as a family on lawn-and-grounds cleanup days.

"Then, one Saturday evening seven years ago, we hired a babysitter and joined my parents at a special program at St. Thomas More's auditorium. A knowledgeable priest from San Francisco gave a talk about Satanism. Many parents were interested in the subject because of reports that teens in the Houston area were becoming involved in Satanic groups. Jed seemed spellbound, especially by the slides the speaker presented. He began reading extensively on the subject, and he and Will spent many hours at the library. Jed started a special study group he calls the Last Saturday Night Club, which happens on the last Saturday of every month. I make refreshments for them, but wives aren't invited. I tried to express my concerns about what was happening to our family, but Jed simply stared at me, looking mean. He never hit me, though he frightened me. I thought he might hit me. He was no longer the man I married. How could such coldness and pain infect us? His eyes changed and became angry and dark. I was scared, because Will's eyes started to look the same. Mothers shouldn't have to see that look in their child's eyes. He is only twelve, Sister."

Sister Andrea listened with quiet intensity. She handed Mary Powers some Kleenex. Andrea felt like hugging Mary. Andrea carefully explained the treatment plan in detail, gave Mary a copy to give to Jed, and made a follow-up appointment.

CHAPTER 5

So This Is Therapy?

Tom reached the small psychotherapy office at St. Thomas More School thirty minutes before his first appointment with Will Powers. Tom pondered his child-therapy experiences during his psychiatric training and the forty years since. Children rarely asked to see a psychiatrist or psychotherapist. If one did, the psychiatrist needed to pay special attention.

Tom recalled several such kids. In each instance, the young person was significantly depressed, homicidal, or suicidal. Usually, a parent brought in the young person at the recommendation of a family physician, teacher, school, court, or law-enforcement authority. Will was a usual referral in the sense that he'd been referred by the school, but he was unusual due to the murky atmosphere surrounding his home situation and the delicate, multifaceted treatment plan.

Establishing trust and rapport with children and adolescents wasn't easy. With young children, Tom used art therapy or play therapy, such as crayon drawing, puppet play, or doll play. Tom sensed that Will required a departure from traditional child-therapy intervention. Many only children who were troubled were *adultified*, acting like adults on the surface. Will might participate in a talking cure like an adult, but the twelve year old would be there, too. Hiding in plain sight but well defended.

Sister Mary Agnes knocked on the door at exactly eleven o'clock. She said, "Will, this is Dr. Tolman. He's the doctor we decided it was necessary for you to talk to in order to stay at our school. You can walk over to the cafeteria after your talks with him are finished."

After Sister Mary Agnes left, Tom invited Will to sit.

"I'd rather stand," Will said, "so I can look at the books on the shelves or look out the window as we talk. Is that okay?"

What a clever tactic to gain control, Tom thought. *It's more than some tactics acquired by older children who spend most of their time around adults. He's like a pseudo adult. Though he's alert and obsequious on the surface, anger shows in his eyes.*

Tom said, "It's important for you to be comfortable for our talks. Sitting isn't the rule in therapy."

Will stared intently at the book titles, and said, "These books are all the same old church books. My dad and I find more interesting books at libraries."

Be careful, Tom, Tolman warned himself. *It's important to explore the words, ideas, and associations that he brings to the interview and not just your questions. Such brilliant questions might lead the witness too much. In the process, it could fracture small glimmers of rapport.*

The diagnostic interview process of associative anamnesis involved circling back to Will's recollections, thoughts, words, and topics of discussion for exploration. Tom had to focus on what was of central importance to Will. If he was to form any interpretation or confrontation with Will about his life, it had to be anchored in trust, rapport, and an accurately empathic atmosphere in therapy. Truth about the self was often painful. When it was tolerated at all, it was in small doses.

"What books do you like to read?" Tom asked.

Will's eyes flashed a dark warning, as he calmly said, "My dad says we don't share our special books with anyone except special friends or club members."

"What club is that?"

Will's eyes flashed angrily again. "I told you we don't share stuff like that!"

"Will," Tom said gently, "it helps me to know about your interests, activities, and what you want to learn."

Will walked along the bookshelves on both walls and read all the titles, which took a while. When he finished, he sat staring intently at Tom. They sat in silence for a long time. Tom thought of the different types of silence in psychotherapy. Unlike angry, sad, lonely, confused, frightened, or bored silences, the one between himself and Will seemed respectful and relatively comfortable. Did it contain a precious glimmer of rapport? Any more questions from Tom might stir more anger, annoyance, and resistance in Will. Few children or teens could tolerate silence for long during a therapy session, but Will seemed completely at ease and glanced at magazines on the table or gazed out the window. The forty-five minute session ended when Tom announced their time was up for the day. Will nodded when Tom said he'd see him again on Thursday. Tom felt pretty good about his first session with the boy.

Will trudged toward the school cafeteria, his thoughts cascading. Dr. Tolman was stupid and weak like the nuns and priests. All adults were stupid except his dad and the men at the Last Saturday Night Club. The weakest of all was his mother, but at least she made sandwiches for the club meetings.

Will wondered if he should talk to his father about Dr. Tolman and decided against it, because his dad had a lot of reading and planning to do for the next club meeting. Dad became angry if his reading and planning time was interrupted. He was fierce about his anger when he needed it. Maybe someday, Will would set the doctor's car on fire. Even find a way to kill him, or at least hurt him bad.

* * * * * * *

After a bag lunch in the St. Thomas teachers' lounge, Tom walked to his car for the short trip to his office. He had several more patients to see before his weekly workout at the health club and an hour at the golf driving range.

Tom loved his MGB. The solid, little, silver-gray sports car had been his delight for many years. On those few treasured, cool, crisp, clear Houston days in the fall and spring, he lowered the convertible top and enjoyed the breeze through his hair as he drove. He often spent a whole weekend driving around the Texas countryside with the top down. His favorite spots were Enchanted Rock near Fredericksburg, Rayburn Lake near Jasper, and the Shoot on the Comal River in New Braunfels. The morning fog didn't allow him to put down the top on Silver B, but he considered it.

Then he noticed writing on the plastic rear window. Big block letters formed the words STUPID, YOU WILL DIE.

He tried to clean it off with a tissue, but all he did was smudge the black lipstick.

Driving to his office, he thought, *So much for a good first therapy session, Tolman. That little punk. Does he even sense how much I cherish my Silver B? Maybe he didn't do it.*

His intuition was seldom wrong. Should he confront Will at their next session? Often, the most difficult thing for a good therapist to do in such a situation was a resounding nothing.

He decided to confer with Andrea first, but he'd probably wait and see what came up naturally at the next session. It was pleasant to picture Andrea in his mind's eye. Such collaborative intimacy must be anathema to Will's recent experiences of a man and woman in a family. Besides, Tom looked forward to time with Andrea away from the St. Thomas More campus.

* * * * * *

Andrea wore a light-blue habit with a white lace collar. The outfit revealed as much as it concealed. Tom was pleased with the softer feminine tone. He found himself increasingly attracted to her sexually. Brought up a moderately attuned Catholic by his mother, Jenny, he wasn't distressed by his attraction to a nun. They met at a quiet French restaurant called San Michelle's on Richmond Avenue, some distance from the parish. As they waited for dinner, Tom described the situation with Will. Andrea listened intently, then asked, "Are you completely sure it was Will? We have occasional episodes of graffiti at St. Tom's. This incident occurs at a crucial phase of our effort to treat Will and his family."

Tom, feeling tired, said, "Andrea, if I don't mention it at all to Will, I'll be perceived as weak. If I bring it up aggressively, I might destroy the tiny amount of rapport I may have with him. This tightrope is stressful. I care about Will, but my anger at him and his father is getting in the way."

She smiled patiently, saying, "The key question is, can you contain and channel your anger and eventually help Will explore his own anger and pain?"

I'm in love with a nun who speaks truth to a shrink, he thought.

Tom said, "I don't know what I'll say to him tomorrow, but it's been good discussing the situation with you today."

I'm picturing Andrea and me as Will's psychotherapeutic godparents.

As they left the restaurant parking lot, a gentle breeze tousled her hair. They paused as she took out her car key, then she grasped his hand tightly.

Andrea said, "I really enjoyed our dinner. No matter what the topic, our talks are always important. Frankly, I wish we had met many years ago. You might have altered my career path."

When she giggled, he knew it was about her quip. The lingering handhold or handshake was enjoyable. Both squeezed equally. Had anyone noticed? Who the hell cared?

He blushed slightly, keeping his eyes on hers. "Let's do this again. Everything about our friendship is important to me."

He wanted to say more, to kiss and hold her, but that had to wait, though not too long. Andrea drove west into a fading sunset on Richmond Avenue. Tom lowered the Silver B's top and drove down Greenbriar toward his condo near Rice University, with the breeze in his hair. He felt younger and less lonely. A verse from church long ago came to mind: *The Lord God said, 'It isn't good for the man to be alone. I need to make a suitable partner for him.'* [Genesis 2:18]

CHAPTER 6

Evil's Shadows Appear

Tom felt significant anxiety as he awaited Will's arrival for their Thursday appointment. He wondered why he felt so anxious about a psychotherapy session with a twelve-year-old boy. Was he confusing his own conflicts or problems with Will's? He spent six long years and about $132,000 on his own personal analysis. He joined a twice-weekly therapy group for a year after finishing individual psychoanalysis. The leader was an experienced psychoanalyst as well as a skilled group psychotherapist. The group members were all professional therapists. They were committed to highly confidential, no-holds-barred, truth-confronting work with each other.

The reason for group therapy was that Tom wanted other perceptive therapists to give him honest feedback about all problem areas and potential blind spots they might see in his therapy work with patients. He occasionally consulted with the group leader when he sensed difficulties in work with his therapy patients, or *analysands*.

The group and the leader frequently confronted Tom about his tendency to be intimidated by men he initially perceived as charismatic, powerful, or angry. Tom remembered the cold, angry look on Jed Powers's face before he abruptly shut the door in his and Andrea's faces. He also remembered his father's angry glower when Tom refused to attend seminary. He wanted to be a physician, with or without his father's help.

He forced himself back to thoughts about Will Powers. Tom suddenly realized he contained the anxiety, anger, and fear Will brought to his recent therapy sessions. Will appeared calm, confident, strong, and in control. Such apparently positive strength seemed in direct proportion to the degree that Tom contained the toxic stew of negative feelings in Will's unconscious mind. If Will felt comfortable, the noble therapist suffered. Tom, like a shaman in a Navajo sweat lodge, had moist armpits to prove it.

Damn! I am the "sin-eater" for Will Powers.

He felt tired before Will arrived and thought of the R-word again. Then he heard a knock on his door.

"I'm here, Dr. Tolman," Will announced.

"Good morning, Will."

Will ignored the chairs and walked near the bookshelves, saying, and "Same books?"

Does he think that because he was critical of the books at a recent session, they'd be removed or changed? Tom wondered. *The little prick. Pretty damn grandiose.*

"What books would you like us to have here, Will?'

Will thought for a minute. With a mixture of unctuousness and a smirk, he said,

"You should have medieval history books. You don't need all

these ones about church history. There are other history writers, not just church people."

Tom said, "This is a Catholic school, so teachers and priests would naturally have church history books. Your teachers or the St. Thomas school librarian can locate other history books for you."

Will scowled, saying, "They don't want to hear other ideas about history, and neither do you, Dr. Tolman."

Tom said, "What ideas do you think I wouldn't want to hear?"

Will pronounced, "Ideas like there's no God and no heaven or hell. Having fun and doing whatever you want is God. That's what's good. When you die, you're gone. You rot, and worms eat you and dump you back into the dirt. Jesus didn't save anybody. He just died. That's all. See, Dr. Tolman, I can tell by your face that you don't like me telling you real history. I want to write a book someday. I'll call it *Real History, Not Fake History*. Most people are fakes. They're scared about dying, and they're scared of serious truth. I have fun watching people's faces when I tell them the serious truth, especially scared little kids at school who have wimpy parents."

Tom worked to remain calm, but his inner thoughts swirled. Will was amazingly blunt. Did he have deep thoughts, or was that merely brainwashing? He sounded bitter.

Tom confronted Will with, "Are you scared about dying, Will? When Sister Andrea and Sister Mary Agnes asked me to see you for counseling, they mentioned you performed funerals for dead birds and squirrels on the playground. Some of the little kids were scared by what you said. Also, you hurt Penny Paulsen with your pencil stab."

"I'm not scared!" Will said, bristling. "Those stupid kids thought the dead birds would go to bird heaven. That's the stupid kind of stuff the priests and nuns teach them. I was just trying to give a regular earth burial ceremony for the birds. I couldn't let Penny stop me. I told the kids the truth. When we die, we don't go into the sky to heaven. We rot in the ground, and worms help our flesh get absorbed back into the earth. Our bones are hard and take much, much longer to rot. That's the truth, isn't it, Doctor?"

What jolting questions from a twelve year old, he thought. *He naturally lumps me in with the priests and nuns here at St. Toms, whom he dislikes and disrespects. His questions knife right into my own ambivalent, struggling, wannabe Christian soul. Years ago, I got beyond the grandiosity of my village atheist self, but I've stumbled along ever since as a fashionably agnostic shrink. That works among colleagues and most patients, but not alone at night with myself—and not here and now.*

Tom said to Will, "You're right about the flesh, bones, and chemicals of our bodies, and those of the squirrels and birds, too. But some people, especially strongly believing Christian people, think that between the molecules of our brains and bodies there's a spirit or soul. Believers have faith that after our bodies die, our spirits or souls live forever. Some scientists have done studies they think prove it. You and I can read those and discuss them sometime if you want."

Will sneered, saying, "I don't believe that stuff, and neither does my dad. He says I should study my other subjects, but I don't have to believe the boring Christian crap."

Tom took notes about looking for the studies about souls, near-death experiences, and similar things in his seminar notes. He must reread David Turell's fine book, *Science vs. Religion: The 500 Year War: Finding God in the Heat of the Battle.* Turell's book could become important bibliotherapy for Will.

They sat in silence until their time was up. Sometimes, saying nothing was the most important intervention for a therapist and an important communication from the patient. Tom felt the silence was comfortable and soothing. He and Will gazed out the window, where a few leaves blew about in the fall breeze.

Will appeared uneasy but sat quietly.

"Our time's up for today," Tom said. "I think we had an important talk. See you next time, Will."

Will smirked but didn't reply.

After Will left, Tom felt exhausted and drowsy. He stretched out on the office sofa and slept. He hadn't mentioned the graffiti on the Silver B.

* * * * * *

Children's voices outside on the playground woke him barely in time to drive the short distance to his office in the Rice University Village area. His power nap helped. Will wasn't his only patient, just the most draining.

CHAPTER 7

Enter Jed Powers, Father God

"My name is Jed Powers. The first hour of our Satan club meeting is filled with an educational talk about Satanism. My twelve-year-old son, Will Powers, is allowed to attend that part of the meeting. I want my son to be strong and powerful. Someday he'll attend the whole meeting. I want Will to admire me. Not like my disgust for my damn dad! The real excitement happens in the second hour of our meeting."

Jed Powers typed his talk for the next meeting in bold type on his PC word processor, reading it aloud.

"My dear Last Saturday Night Club members, hear these approved thoughts extracted from the lean, strong meat of Anton Szandor LaVey's writings. I specifically chose his *Satanic Bible*. Listen, you proud men who love and can feel Lucifer's song and dance tonight. Evil is *live* spelled backward. Most people are fools who worship at the altars of their humdrum lives and silly, superstitious, religious commitments."

"Our group is powerful. When we talk about or draw blood

from our animal sacrifices, we see it as evidence of our power, control, and pleasure at being in charge. We don't need to sing hymns about the blood of Jesus washing away our sins. Our only sins occur when we neglect our fun, dominance, and the pleasure taken in our power. Our great deity is Satan. He has figured out the big galactic con job perpetuated by Allah, God, and Yahweh. God spelled backward is dog. Our altar's sacrifices drive the hound of heaven into the muddy swamps of the power of our mockery."

"Feel that power, my members! Feel the power!"

* * * * * * *

Jed Powers always felt good after telling Mary how things were and would be. He hated the name Mary. The mother and the girlfriend of that loser Jesus carried that name. He told Mary she could meet with that do-gooder shrink and his nun friend, but he'd have nothing to do with them. Jed allowed Will to attend St. Thomas but just for the free education and nothing else.

Powers retreated to his special desk in the castle room. He still bristled with rage when he thought of those Catholic hypocrites. Their sick sanctimony reminded him of his father Val, who was named for Prince Valiant, that sick SOB. Val Powers preached one thing and lived another. What a rigid, sick excuse for a life. Jed was glad when he heard his father died, and he didn't attend the funeral. He recalled a pansy priest who once said that hate was more powerful than love. Jed chuckled, sneered, and belched beer.

Jed thought of his first boss at Baylor College of Medicine's Animal Resource Center. At first, the man encouraged Jed to stick to his ambition of entering veterinarian school. Then the hypocrite refused to write a letter of recommendation for Jed's scholarship application. He said Jed lacked accurate empathy, the bastard. What the hell was accurate empathy? No one cared. The only pleasure or good one got was what he grabbed for himself. Only strength brought respect. He loved reading Ayn Rand, especially *Atlas Shrugged*. Brutal selfishness, not love, won real salvation. *Fuck You, Jesus,* he thought.

Bitterness saturated his being like a drenching sweat from hard work in the Houston sun. Leaning back in his comfortable desk chair, Jed imagined the respectful, admiring eyes of his loyal club members on Saturday night. The old saying about a man's home being his castle rang true for Jed in his castle room. Jed knew he had a special talent. He could paraphrase and cite brief quotes from Anton Szandor LaVey's *The Satanic Bible* to form a unique, powerful mixture for his presentation to the Last Saturday Night Club. Jed was a self-appointed LaVey scribe, lieutenant, and local Houston satanic prophet, and he loved it.

He carefully chose the seven members of the club for their seriousness about Satanic theology, ability to keep secrets, and loyalty. They were light-blue-collar guys with steady jobs, but they were bored with their humdrum, day-in-day-out, workaday world. They looked forward to the Last Saturday Night Club as a special form of excitement. They basked in a sense of quiet superiority that Jed helped promote. He was their special leader and Satanic father figure.

* * * * * *

Jed's mahogany desk sat in the corner of the club's meeting room.

High above was the domed skylight that allowed sacred Satanic moonlight to fall on some meetings. Just below the dome were windows in a ring that captured moonlight, too. The desk drawers contained his red, hooded Satan robe, gold dagger, and gold sash. All drawers were locked.

A mahogany-framed letter of appreciation from Anton LaVey and Jed's carefully prepared lectures and club rules were kept locked away until the club's meeting time. He often took the sacred objects from their drawers to admire between meetings.

Seven comfortable chairs sat in a semicircle. Jed's special wing-backed chair faced them and sat to one side of the altar, which had a thick, three-by-five-foot mahogany top on a solid granite base. On the altar was mounted a hand-carved image of a goat, as Satan's head, which was visible from the members' chairs.

Sunk into the wood was a gold basin large enough for a small animal. He spent many joyful hours sculpting the head and polishing the altar with loving care each month.

Though he had already memorized it, he returned to his desk to reread the final draft of his sermon for the next club meeting. When he finished, he tried on his hood while looking in the mirror on the wall behind the altar, and practiced what he called his fierce, earthy smile. He tried to mimic LaVey's visage, which he saw in a book. He felt the twinge of an erection under his robe. Life was good in the castle room, his castle.

CHAPTER 8

In Search of a Father's Love

Will wished his father spent more time with him. He remembered when his dad used to read to him when he was a little boy. He imagined snuggling close to his father on the big, comfortable chair in the living room with his dad's big, muscled arm around him. He recalled the scent of daddy's Old Spice cologne.

In recent times, his father always stayed in his castle office in the meeting room of the Last Saturday Night Club. Will knew his dad did important work out there, but he missed the special closeness. At least he had his special friend, Jake, who always listened and understood.

Will enjoyed trips to libraries and bookstores with his father. He also enjoyed reading about how to raise rabbits. They bred many rabbits, but Will was allowed to keep only two at any one time. His two rabbits were named Whitey and Brownie. Whitey was completely white, while Brownie was brown with two small white spots on his chest.

Will loved his rabbits and took good care of them. They were soft and cuddly, never mean or fussy. He was strict about them and very protective. All the others were sold to pet stores or donated to the Baylor College of Medicine. Dad said student and research doctors used the rabbits for important research. Dad was the boss of the Baylor research lab.

The third thing he liked to do with his dad was attend the meetings of the Last Saturday Night Club, which his dad led. Will was allowed to attend the first hour of the meeting. The friendly club members thanked him when he helped bring in sandwiches and drinks. After the first hour, Will had to go to his room upstairs in the rear of the house, far from the special meeting room. The second part of the meeting was secret. Dad said that when Will turned eighteen, he could be a full member of the club and attend the entire meeting, but eighteen seemed too distant—like his father recently.

It was the last Saturday night in September, and Will was excited. Dad gave a good talk about the history of Satanism and the black mass, which sounded much better and more fun than St. Thomas's mass.

Will was walking upstairs after leaving the meeting when he remembered he forgot to give Whitey and Brownie their carrot snacks. He got the carrots and went to the backyard door near the rabbit hutch, just off the breezeway along the house. He fed Whitey his carrot and cuddled him briefly. Brownie resisted cuddling a bit, and when he held Brownie up to the light from the breezeway window, Will saw he had only one white spot on his chest.

He put the rabbit back into the hutch. Something was wrong. That wasn't Brownie! He considered interrupting the meeting, but his dad told him never to do that. He'd ask his dad the next day.

As Will entered the breezeway, he heard a shriek like a terrified baby through the thick meeting room door. He had read about rabbits making sounds like that on rare occasions, when they were in pain and really scared. Will felt numb, and his stomach hurt like a knife was in it. His vision narrowed until it was like looking through binoculars backward. His palms sweated, his heart raced, and he felt sick.

He stumbled into the backyard. A ladder leaned against the meeting room wall, where Dad had been painting the trim around the windows high up on the turret of the castle room. He climbed carefully and quietly until he looked through the window.

The club members stood around a mahogany table that resembled a church altar, but it had a carved goat on top with a Satanic pentagram carved on its belly. They wore red robes with hoods and black cloth belts around their waists. Dad's belt was gold.

He saw Brownie tied belly-up on the altar. The rabbit struggled and screamed, but metal straps held him tightly. The club members sang and chanted words Will couldn't make out.

Dad plunged a gold dagger into Brownie's chest, and another member collected blood in a gold cup. The weird smile on Dad's face made Will want to vomit. Trembling and sobbing, he felt hot urine running down his legs. It was like being in a scary black-and-white TV movie without the sound. His tennis shoes partially filled with cooling piss.

He barely made it down the ladder. His mother's bedroom door was closed, and there was no light on in the room. Will put his wet clothes in the bathroom and went straight to bed.

Will said to himself.

"Why the hell would dad do that to Brownie? He works with animals. He helps me get my pet rabbits. Dad told me he once wanted to be a vet. Vets help animals, they don't fuckin' hurt them!"

Jake shook his head. "I can't believe this."

Will never saw Jake cry before. At least he did it silently and didn't sob like Will. Repeatedly, he tried to picture Brownie screaming, but his mind always went numb, unable to form the images from a short time earlier. Will sobbed and shook until he fell asleep. Jake fell asleep at the same moment as Will.

CHAPTER 9

Will's Therapy Takes Hold

Will didn't show up for his Tuesday appointment. Tom checked with Andrea and learned he hadn't been to school Monday or Tuesday. Apparently, he was home sick with a stomachache.

Andrea tried to set up an appointment with Mr. and Mrs. Powers for a parents' meeting. Mary said Jed refused to come, but she would attend alone.

On Thursday, Andrea had to escort Will to his session with Tom. He was ten minutes late. Once in the room, Will paced, sweeping his hands through his black hair, spitting out words.

"I hate this therapy crap! My dad says I don't have to do this."

Tom calmly said, "We wrote your parents a letter explaining that you had to attend therapy to keep coming to school at St. Thomas. Sister Andrea and I want to meet your parents face-to-face to discuss your therapy and communication issues in your family."

Will glared, saying, "My father's strong and smart and doesn't need therapy crap!"

Tom took a deep, slow breath and said, "Will, if your dad was strong, smart, and a good parent, he would come for a meeting about your education and therapy. What's he so afraid to talk about? I think you're angry and sad about your dad. I think you put those feelings on me and your teachers. The priests here are called fathers. I think you put your anger on me when you wrote *stupid* on my car window. I want to help you understand where your anger comes from and what to do with it."

Will moved toward the office door. Tom grabbed his shoulder firmly, though Will squirmed and pulled away. Tears flooded down his cheeks.

"Take your fucking hands off me!" he shouted. "I'll report you for child abuse, you queer, crazy person's shrink doctor!"

Tom looked into the boy's raging, tearful eyes.

"Time is up for this short session today, but we need to talk more about this stuff at next Tuesday's session."

Will slammed the door. Tom watched him walk toward the main school building, gesturing as if talking to a companion beside him on the path, or perhaps to himself.

Tom always allowed at least five, sometimes fifteen, minutes after therapy sessions. It wasn't just for phone calls or record keeping. If charged for that time, just like collaboration time with teachers or other therapists, insurance companies would never pay for it. That penny-wise, pound-foolish approach fed into the incredibly superficial contemporary psychotherapy wasteland. Psychotherapy was steadily, slowly, and relentlessly becoming shallow. Quick fixes, formulaic nostrums, and one-size-fits-all psychological Band-Aids prevailed.

For Tom, the precious five minutes before and after a session allowed him to process what might occur or just happened. He could explore his inner personal feelings and apply them to his understanding of the patient and where treatment might be heading, or what intervention he might choose. The most difficult clinical decision often was to say or do nothing.

The intensity of Will's anger bewildered him. If his theory that Will was projecting anger and rage from his father, Tom and all the authorities at St. Thomas were his transference targets. The displacement of rage at a father onto other adult authority figures was the textbook definition of transference.

As he explored that theory in his mind, he became calm and peaceful within, which told him the theory was right. Despite the intensity, therapy with Will was making progress. Will felt pain. Like physical pain, psychological pain was protective because it sounded a warning. It called attention to the problem for the healer and the healed. Will's brimming anger and pain meant that a crisis in his therapy was near.

The Chinese character for crisis meant both *danger* and *opportunity*. Tom needed to be alert.

* * * * * * *

Tom saw patients at his office until three o'clock. He had a one-hour break due to a cancellation, and he realized he left his briefcase in Sister Andrea's office at St. Thomas that morning. As Tom walked toward the school offices, he saw Will sitting alone on a bench beside the baseball field.

Tom walked up to him. "May I sit with you?"

Will glared at him through slightly bloodshot eyes. "What are you doing here, head doctor?"

Tom sat down without waiting for an invitation. "I left some things at the office this morning and came back for them. Why are you still here, Will? School was out awhile ago."

Will stared at his well-worn sneakers, picked his nose, and said, "I like to sit here sometimes and think, especially when there are no stupid kids or teachers around."

Tom removed his sport coat and slung it over the bench. With his hands in his pockets, he slouched back and gazed up at the billowy clouds drifting by in the fall afternoon. They provided occasional shade before bright sunlight shone through again. He left his jacket and walked to the well-used, scratched, dented pay phone near the baseball backstop, catching his secretary just before she left for the day and asking her to cancel his last three patients.

Tom returned to sit beside Will, who still looked angry but seemed more sad than anything else. Tom resumed his slouching and cloud-gazing.

"What are you looking at, head doctor?" Will asked.

Tom said, "I like to watch clouds float by and imagine what they look like. They can be mountains, animals, boats, flowers—anything my mind thinks up."

Will sported a rare grin, saying, "That's weird, Shrink Doctor."

Tom said, "Try it and see what you find."

Will looked up for awhile, then began, "I see a white rabb…."

He leaped to his feet saying, "I have to go home." He trotted toward his old bike with tears in his eyes.

Tom said, "Will, stay and talk!"

Will stopped for a second like someone caught in a game of freeze tag. He quickly wiped away tears with a wrinkled red bandana plucked from the back pocket of his dirty jeans. Looking intently at Tom, Will asked, "Can you keep a secret and never tell it?"

Tom said, "Keeping personal secrets is one of the main things I do during my work, but telling secrets depends on if someone is in danger."

Will walked back slowly and sat beside Tom again. They sat in silence, watching clouds. Will's eyes filled with tears again, and he turned slightly away.

Will spoke tersely, "I can't believe dad did that to Brownie," he said. "Brownie was screaming. My stomach hurt so bad, and my head felt like I was spinning on a ride at AstroWorld. I peed my pants. I almost fell off the ladder Saturday night."

Tom took a deep, slow, silent breath and sat with his ear cocked, ready to listen. *Don't push the river,* he told himself.

Slowly, haltingly, and with occasional uncharacteristic stammering, Will recounted the events at the meeting of the Last Saturday Night Club. Tom, stunned, had cottonmouth, and his neck and forehead were tense. When his story was finished, Will sobbed, clenching and unclenching his fists. Finally, he grew quiet.

Tom said, "It's normal to feel sad and mad about what your dad did. Did you feel like punching him?"

Will blurted, "I wanted to bang on the door and stop him. I wanted to take Brownie to an animal doctor, but I'd have been in bad trouble. You haven't seen my dad's eyes when he's real mad. They're scary."

Tom said quietly, "I've seen his eyes, and they're scary, but I'm not afraid of your father. I want to help you, so he won't hurt your pets or you. Maybe even help your dad."

Will jumped up, saying, "You won't tell my mother, my teachers, or the police about my dad, will you?" His eyes filled with a mixture of anger, fear, and sadness. He was so tense that his neck veins bulged as he stood and looked down on Tom. Clouds thickened in the autumn sky.

Will edged toward his bike, staring at Tom, saying, "You gonna tell?"

Tom said, "I agree to keep our secret for now, but we need to talk a lot more at our next therapy session about how we can change the scary situation in your family."

Will trotted to his bike. As he rode off, he gestured and spoke to someone seemingly on another bike beside him, but he rode alone.

Tom gazed at the armada of darkening clouds drifting across the west Houston sky, hoping for hints about answers to his raft of questions.

CHAPTER 10

Benevolent Authority as Therapy

They sat in a corner booth sipping fresh coffee at Jerry's Donut Shop. Andrea's blue eyes mirrored and resonated with her sky-colored habit. They sparkled as she listened intently to Tom's account of his meeting with Will.

"Andrea, I'm flummoxed," Tom confessed. "I don't know whether to call the police, DCYF, the Society for the Prevention of Cruelty to Animals, or my lawyer. The only positive thing about this is that Will shows dawning awareness of his father's cruelty. That issue alone has complicated emotions attached. There are pitfalls for his therapy."

Andrea said, "Is Will, or perhaps his mother, in danger?"

Tom replied, "I really don't know, but I'm worried. I know that flagrant psychological abuse of Will has occurred at his father's hands. It's also clear that the Marshalls fear for their daughter and grandson. I'm counting on Will not to tell his father I know about this. His trust in me to keep it secret is intense. I implied I would until our next therapy session. We both know that DCYF is perpetually swamped with cases. Many are more serious than the Powerses.' But, by law, we're obligated to report this to them."

Andrea added, "Yes, within forty-eight hours."

Tom continued, "If we report this hastily, it might tip off Jed Powers and stir his paranoid core. It might even trigger antisocial or violent behavior. My first thought is that we need the Houston police and DCYF. My second thought is that the police might laugh at us."

Andrea said, "There's no way HPD would laugh, Tom. I'll call Detective Mark Lane, a member of our congregation. I know him well from a committee on drug abuse on which we both served. He's dedicated, a straight shooter, and very experienced."

Tom said, "Good idea. I'll call Harry Marshall. We might ask the Marshalls to have Will and Mary stay with them when we confront Jed. Let's talk soon. Detective Lane's input seems crucial."

They agreed to meet at Jerry's Donut Shop the following afternoon. As she got up to leave, Andrea squeezed Tom's hand. He felt like a blushing but pleased college boy, and his thoughts wandered.

He hadn't dated anyone seriously in over a year, but the rush of arousal was more than mid-life hormones. Andrea was loving and lovely, and she stirred his aging hormone levels.

Tom felt that Freud must've scratched his brilliant head and stretched his thinking to try to answer the timeless riddle, *What do women want?*

Tom wondered what men and women sought. Where were they headed when they performed their strange mating dances? It was more than an elemental, dominant quest for orgasm and pleasure. The tendrils of boredom eventually found fertile soil in modern, civilized life and sometimes led down exciting, erotic trails in transient searches for a way to end boredom. Such rabbit trails of desire tempted an irrational array of daring suspensions of sexual boundaries and good judgment. Moans of sexual excitement fended off boredom only briefly.

How successful would a movie or modern novel be if it described a loving, sharing, caring, committed couple who never contemplated an exciting affair? Infidelity often drew excitement from flirtation with a brink of lies, deceit, and real risk of divorce. Was it just a restless, futile search for one's star-crossed other half? The search for the utopia of intimacy never lasted, but was seldom abandoned.

Tom felt that one hint at an answer came from the mystery described to him by Dr. Sukawatana, an older, wiser colleague he knew during his psychiatric residency training. A Buddhist, he blended Freudian notions of the unique individual with Buddhist efforts to downplay individualism, forming an interesting, paradoxical blend.

Suki's wife and family were in Thailand, awaiting his return after his three-year residency training. Suki loved his wife and missed her. Tom liked the man, and, knowing of his loneliness, often invited him to dinner on weekends.

On one of these evenings, after Tom and his ex-wife entertained Suki, he walked Suki to his car.

Before getting in, Suki turned and said, "Tom, thank you for this evening. I've come to love you and Joan, but can I give you advice?"

Tom nodded and became more alert.

Suki regarded him intently. "Love Joan with your heart, not just your head."

They paused and leaned on Suki's old, rusty Ford Falcon. Suki added, "I miss my lovely Wan every day, as my memory pictures join my heart songs about her. She delivers babies in a Bangkok hospital every day. I love to think of her with those new babies and our babies, who aren't babies anymore. I want you to also know that Wan and I in our souls know that in the next life, we may not be together. We long to be husband and wife in the dawn beyond death's powerful mystery, but we can't know with certainty. We might not even complete this present life together, so we value our separate paths of growth and experience. As we both become very old, our love will lead us to attend different temples, so our souls don't become so fearful that we get inextricably bound together. Enough of my pontifications. Don't think me rude."

Tom felt jolted with wonder, like the first time his analyst helped him interpret the meaning and action implications of his dream life.

Tom said to Suki, "Far from rude, you've given me a gift of wisdom and important things to think about, and, I hope, to feel about."

They hugged, then Suki's car rattled off toward his apartment near the Texas Medical Center.

Tom often recalled that encounter. He tried to apply Suki's wisdom to the lively spirit of Andrea Albright. Her mind and heart ran lively circles around love-struck Tom Tolman, but he enjoyed the dance.

* * * * * * *

Tom called Harry Marshall, who was worried about his grandson and daughter. He was convinced that Mary was so mesmerized or afraid of Jed that she wouldn't leave the house even under the present circumstances. Harry and Monica would be glad to have Will and Mary stay with them. He added that Monica would soon take Mary out to lunch and would try to make her understand how concerned they were about her blind spots regarding her husband. Tom agreed to stay in touch.

The following morning, Tom walked to Jerry's Donut Shop. Andrea sat at a table beside a tall, powerfully built, sandy-haired man with a boyish grin. Tom noticed a faint bulge halfway up his left chest under his attractive leather sport coat. Tom got his coffee and approached their table.

"Tom," Andrea said, "I'd like you to meet Detective Mark Lane. Mark, this is Dr. Tom Tolman."

Lane's handshake was firm without being bone-crushing. Tom immediately felt comfortable with the man's confidence but heard a faint whisper from his past.

His analyst once said, long ago, "Build trust carefully and slowly, so it lasts."

Andrea quickly got down to business. "Tom, Mark shares our concern about Will's safety and psychological well-being around Jed Powers. Mark has also pointed out that we don't have sufficient probable cause for a search of their home or to confront Jed, but we could make an anonymous call to DCYF concerning what Will told you."

"Doc," Mark said, "I could talk to a judge with jurisdiction about a search warrant, but I know what he or she would say—no sufficient probable cause. Another approach would be Plan B. After you call in a report of abuse, I could accompany the DCYF investigator when she visits the Powers house to interview Will and his parents. Unless Will speaks about what happened in the Last Saturday Night Club meeting room, I couldn't look around the premises without a search warrant. Usually, the DCYF worker interviews and examines each child separately in his room, then the parents separately, then the whole family together. Such an approach would put enormous pressure on Will."

Tom said, "Not to mention what it would stir up in his father. What are our other options?"

Lane answered, "It would take me or a detective colleague too long to infiltrate Jed's Satanic cult group. Plan C could happen soon after Plan B. On the last Saturday night of this month, you and I could directly observe what they're doing."

Tom asked, "Is that legal? How would we accomplish that?"

Lane went further. "The situation is unusual, but my captain and I are close. I can convince him that special investigative measures are needed in such a unique situation. Hopefully, Captain Smith could get us a search warrant to take along, just in case. We could use the same ladder Will used. I've got a high-resolution camera that fits in my shirt pocket."

After some pointed procedural questions and discussions, Tom agreed to call in a complaint to DCYF immediately after his next session with Will. Mark would tell the social worker of his interest in accompanying her during her visit to the Powers home.

Andrea closed their meeting with a prayer.

"Father, we must have your unique presence in the next days and weeks. Special wisdom is needed, as we tread on Solomon's turf around Will Powers and his family. I pray that Powers hasn't totally hardened his heart like the pharaoh of ancient Egypt."

* * * * * * *

Will was slightly early for his next therapy session, and he wasn't alone. Mary Powers was of average height and slightly overweight, but still attractive. The frown lines on her face were overworked, which detracted from her good looks. She stared intently at Tom as she accepted the offered chair. Will, as usual, stood and paced near the bookshelves.

"Dr. Tolman," she said, "Will tells me that he didn't like you at first, but recently you had a good talk. I've tried to talk to you and Sister Andrea like my mother urges, but my husband doesn't understand psychology or psychiatry. He'd be angry if he knew I was speaking with you. I feel ashamed for not responding to your letters; Jed tore one up in front of Will and me."

Will glanced at her with an expression that combined fear and anger.

"Mrs. Powers, I'm glad you're here," Tom said. "Right after my session with Will today, I plan to report your husband to the Department of Child Protective Services, as I'm required to do by law."

Mary looked stunned.

Will glared at Tom and snapped, "You damn head doctor! You promised you'd keep a secret and wouldn't tell. I thought I could trust you! Now I hate you!"

Tom fought off the inner writhing of his old neurotic guilt.

Fifteen-year-old memories flooded through his mind. He had worked hard with the help of his own psychotherapist, Dr. Cal Goldberg, to assert truth without such guilt. When Tom was a boy, his mother, Jenny, seemed to regard anyone's assertiveness as dangerous, and, by spiritual extension, sinful. Tom grew to realize that she and her vintage of Christianity saw all strong emotions as potentially sinful. Intense anger, sexual passion, and the longing for nurturing hugs were suspect unless one was physically ill.

During his personal analytic experience, Tom became aware of how important it was for him to put strong feelings into words and effective actions. People who had successful psychoanalysis carried vivid memories of their analyst like an omnipresent friend or sagacious companion. Analysts called that "self-analysis" or the "self-analytic function." The analyst became a wise, nurturing inner presence in the temporal lobe of the analysand's brain.

Tom once told Goldberg, "When I can put my anger and resentment into spoken words without suppressing or repressing them, particularly resentment toward people who are important to me, I can prevent my suffering from a tension headache or a full-blown migraine."

Tom brought his thoughts back to the present, saying, "Will, what your dad did to your pet, Brownie, was cruel and wrong. Your dad and his Satan club can read, study, and talk about whatever they want, but Texas law says they can't hurt an animal or person. When your dad hurt Brownie and took his blood, that was bad and wrong. It brought pain to you, because you love and care about Brownie. We call what you saw your dad do to Brownie child abuse. Texas law requires me to report him, so he'll stop doing those bad things. It might also make him get help for the sickness inside him that causes crooked thinking and bad behavior."

Will, sitting stiffly on the padded arm of his mother's chair, clenched and unclenched his fists while staring out the window. Tom gave Mary a summary of the scene Will witnessed. The boy didn't resist when she put her arm around him, but he glared at Tom. Tom urged them to tell the truth when DCYF came to their house. He reminded Mary that he and Sister Andrea would keep an invitation open for Jed to meet them. Tom made it clear he wanted Will to keep his next appointments, because they were very important.

He watched them through the window as they left the session and walked toward the school. Mary kept her hand on Will's shoulder, and he didn't resist. Mary had looked worried yet relieved when she left. And, she seemed less depressed.

CHAPTER 11

New Home Visits

Mark Lane worked previously with Jill Saunders of the Texas division of Children, Youth, and Families, and knew that DCYF workers were overworked and often burned out. Jill wasn't one of the typical bleeding-heart social workers. She was feisty and no-nonsense, with an irreverent sense of humor. Her style served as built-in burnout prevention.

Dr. Tolman gave Jill detailed information about what Will told him. Tolman and Sister Andrea shared with Jill their observations of the failed attempt to visit the Powers home.

Jill and Mark visited after Will came home from school. Jill pressed the doorbell. Mary opened the door, and, once they identified themselves, invited them inside.

Jill took Will to his room to talk. Mark and Mary sat sipping coffee at the kitchen table.

Mark said, "Mrs. Powers, after Jill finishes speaking with Will, she'll want to speak with you and Mr. Powers, if that's possible."

Mary Powers said, "Jed's in his study. He's there most of the day and doesn't like being disturbed."

"Can you show me his study?" Mark asked. "I'd like to speak to him."

Mary agreed, but looked worried as they walked from the kitchen down the long, glassed-in breezeway toward the large, turret-shaped room beside the garage. Mary stepped back as Lane knocked on the thick oak door with a sturdy double bolt. Jed opened the door and glared at Lane with bloodshot, angry, watery, and shifty blue-gray eyes.

"Mr. Powers, I'm Detective Mark Lane. Today I'm working with Jill Saunders of Child Protective Services. Jill's interviewing your son, Will, right now. Then she'll interview you and Mrs. Powers."

"About what?" Jed growled. "I'm working in my office and can't be bothered."

Mark explained, "A complaint has been filed about you with Child Protective Services of Harris County. Your cooperation is important, Mr. Powers."

Jed locked his office door and walked toward the kitchen. Lane and Mary followed, and the three sat in tense silence around the kitchen table, waiting for Jill.

"Mr. Powers, do you work at home?" Mark asked.

Jed said, "Sometimes I do research here. I work part-time at the animal research labs at Baylor College of Medicine. I take care of the animals the doctors use for research and teaching medical students."

Jill Saunders, entering the kitchen, accepted a cup of coffee from Mary before getting down to business.

Jill said, "Mr. Powers, Will's therapist at school indicated that you exposed Will to cruel treatment of his pet rabbit during your men's club ritual. Will was very upset. His therapist, Dr. Tolman, thinks it traumatized Will."

Jed flushed, and his hands shook slightly as he said, "That's nonsense. Did Will say that about me?"

Jill responded neutrally. "Will wouldn't talk about it, but he was upset when I brought it up. He had tears in his eyes and looked angry."

Jed retorted, "Of course he's upset! You accused me of something ridiculous! I want

both of you out of here right now. I'm calling my lawyer."

Mark Lane gave his card to Jed and Mary, saying, "We need to talk further, Mr. Powers. We'll leave you now and let you give this situation careful thought before we return, or you must come to my office at HPD."

As Mark drove Jill back to her office, she said, "That guy gives me the creeps. Any father in his position would be defensive, but I knew he was lying. Do you think Will and Mary are in danger?"

Lane scratched his head thoughtfully.

"Jed has controlled, frightened, and intimidated Mary and Will for a long time. I don't think they're in immediate danger, but we need to expedite our investigation. I hope Mary and Will decide to live with her parents for a while like Dr. Tolman suggested."

Jill said, "I'll see my boss immediately."

Mark dropped Jill off, and drove to HPD to meet with his captain.

Mark Lane had known Captain Randy Smith for twenty-eight years. They liked and respected each other and had covered each other's backs in some tough situations. Smith called Judge Hartwell. It took a half hour to get a search warrant for Mark Lane to investigate the Powers home.

Judge Hartwell called Jill Saunders, Jill'ssupervisor, and Tom Tolman to support the application for a search warrant. They were fortunate to get such a document on a Friday afternoon. There were a few caring lawyers and judges in Houston, and all needed better press.

CHAPTER 12

Satan Gets the Drop on Helpers

Mark and Tom discussed their proposed eavesdropping on the Last Saturday Night Club's next meeting. They planned to arrive at the house at 8:15 P.M. If Will was home, he should have been dismissed from the club meeting by then.

Mark had a patrolman check the area recently, and there were no dogs nearby that might bark at strangers. The only light on the property was a small one, out front near the mailbox.

As the planning went forward, Tom felt like a kid preparing for a juicy but scary Halloween prank. They decided to wear dark-blue sweat suits, though Lane's had a small *HPD* stitched on the front.

Tom didn't sleep well Friday night, and he felt restless all day Saturday. Through a phone call to Andrea, he learned she was praying frequently for God's presence with them on their mission. The prayer promise and the gentle sound of her voice were more calming than a Valium tablet.

When Lane picked him up at 7:45 P.M., Tom's palms were minimally sweaty and his stomach was less tense. Lane parked his dark-blue, unmarked Ford Crown Victoria across the street and several houses down from the Powers house. As they walked toward the house, Tom noted that the only lights on came from Will's upstairs bedroom and the windows high on the turret-shaped meeting room near the garage. The glassed-in hall between the house, garage, and turret was dark. Several cars and trucks were parked in the driveway and along the street.

They walked around the garage and climbed the low chain-link fence before walking to the ladder that still rested against the wall of the turret-shaped meeting room. Lane climbed it quietly and looked in the window, snapping pictures with his camera.

Tom heard low chanting, organ music, and an eerie keening that reminded him of a baby in distress. Lane came partway down the ladder to show Tom pictures of five men gathered around an altar. All wore hooded robes and chanted while Jed cut up the neck and chest of a white rabbit. The poor animal was tightly bound, and its cries became feeble as Powers drained its blood into a bowl built into the shiny mahogany altar. Tom barely made out the words of the chant. Chills ran up and down his spine.

"Ah, blood, bright, beautiful blood that binds us to Satan and Lucifer's power of lust. We drink of Satan's power."

* * * * * * *

Will stood outside the door to the meeting room, straining to hear what was happening inside. He heard a rabbit scream, and his stomach hurt so much he was ready to throw up. Then he noticed two shadowy figures in the backyard. One was on the ladder. He banged loudly on the door and turned on the backyard floodlights.

"It's Dr. Tolman!" he said to himself out loud. "What's he doing here?"

For a moment he froze, and though he heard more rabbit screams he wanted to protect his father and the club. He grabbed his .22 rifle from the hall closet. Club members streamed out of the club room into the yard just as Will aimed his rifle at the scrambling figures of Tolman and Lane.

Bright lights came on in the glassed-in breezeway. Mark tried to get off the ladder quickly but caught his foot and fell awkwardly. He knocked Tom to the ground and landed on top of him. As they lay under the floodlights, tangled and squirming to stand, Mark tossed his camera into the bushes.

Six men surrounded the pair. Jed aimed a shotgun at the two men and said, "Get up with your hands on your heads."

Tom saw Will standing beside his dad, holding his .22. An element of triumph blended with Will's patented angry smirk.

"Search them, men," said Jed Powers. "Tie their hands behind them and bring them into the club room."

Jed removed his robe and preceded the group into the room.

Probably disposing of the rabbit and blood before Will and the rest of us get in there, Tom thought.

Though Will clearly recognized Tom, he remained silent and kept his gun trained on the two intruders.

Tom and Mark were placed in two folding chairs facing six angry Satanists and Will. Two still wore their robes.

"Jed, this one had a pistol in a shoulder holster," a burly man said.

"Detective Lane, I believe, and you brought along a shrink," Jed said. "How odd. An odd couple?"

The others chuckled.

Jed joked further, cryptically. "Now, what shall we do, call the police?"

They laughed.

"Shall we rough them up before we check their IDs? By the way Will, thanks for spotting these intruders and knocking on the door."

Tom felt stung with a mixture of fear, anger, embarrassment, shame, and sadness.

Though Mark had a bloody lip, he spoke firmly. "Jed, if you look in my sweatpants pocket, you'll see a legal search warrant. After you look at it, I need to get all these men's names and ask you some questions. Will, ask your mother to call Sergeant Jones and Captain Smith at the Houston Police Department."

Jed spoke angrily. "Don't tell my son what to do, Lane! I have some questions for you two. What were you doing snooping around my yard at night? Who do you think you are?"

Tom felt a cold chill, and his neck and stomach tightened. Jed and the Satanists looked very angry. Tom feared he and Lane might be ritually tortured or killed. He thought of Andrea's face and warm smile. He'd been trying hard to move from his recent burnout and depression. He wanted his old love affair with life to return. He feared he faced only cold whispers of death.

No, no, he thought.

Mark Lane knew he had to take charge confidently, or the situation could become dangerous. Mark said, "Jed, you know we're here to check the report that you and this group are cruel to animals and use them in your Satanic rituals. Young Will has been psychologically harmed by this behavior."

Jed Powers snarled, "Our use of animals for our spiritual purposes is lawful, and Will is never present during the ritual phase of our meetings. He'll be there only after he turns eighteen. Also, our use of animals is no different than the medical students at Baylor Med, who use them for physiology and lab experiments and medical research."

Mark pressed, "Jed, you might not have been aware of it, but Will heard a rabbit you were sacrificing screaming in pain,"

Tom said, "He climbed the same ladder we used and saw what you did to his pet Brownie. That was painful and traumatic for him. Certainly you understand that. Your freedom of speech, belief, and worship are sacred, but it's against the law to hurt or sacrifice an animal or person."

The other club members looked at each other and began shuffling their feet. Some stared at the floor.

Jed glared at Tom, and asked, "Will, did you tell the doctor those things?'

Will looked down, then at an empty chair in the corner. His shoulders sagged. Tears came to his eyes, but he didn't answer.

Jed roughly grabbed Will's shoulder. "Will, I asked you a question."

Will nodded and ran from the room. The heavy door slammed. A moment later, a door slammed upstairs in the main house.

Jed slammed Tom's mouth with his fist, saying, "You hypocritical bastard! You went to the cops and didn't even talk to me first."

Though blood oozed from Tom's split lip, he said, "Wait a minute

Jed. We made repeated requests to you to come for sessions with us. We even visited you at home to try to talk to you, and you basically slammed the door on us."

For what seemed a tense eternity, silence filled the room. Several men shuffled their feet. All hung up their robes.

Mark knew he had to take over, saying, "Jed, to assure you of the least amount of trouble tonight, untie us right now. I need to call the local HPD command and get some help interviewing all of you men before any of us can go home. Dr. Tolman and I need to take Will to his grandparents."

"We ain't your prisoners, Lane. You're ours," Jed said.

Rusty, the large, powerful man who tied up the pair, stood. His forehead was sweaty, and the armpits of his Houston Astros T-shirt were soaked. His breath reeked of onions. "Powers, I enjoy these meetings and your talks," he said. "I like your emphasis on healthy selfishness. I spend so much time working to support my family. My wife wants me to give money to our church and the church school. It makes me sick sometimes. In the long run, you're right. LaVey is right. I want to keep our meeting as a separate thing. An oasis of self-love, you called it once. But I didn't know Will had seen and heard our ritual. I got a wife and kids, and I don't want trouble to start here. We all got to keep level heads. I'm for letting these guys loose and cooperating."

Rusty untied Mark and Tom.

Jed grew uncharacteristically red in the face. Through tense lips, he said, "Rusty, I thought we could all stand strong together in this. Are you men going to be dominated by your kids, wives, and these do-gooder hypocrites? Do the rest of you agree with Rusty?"

Jed Powers grabbed Will's .22. The man beside Rusty was short and stocky, with a gray crew cut and a scruffy beard. He wore a Dallas Cowboys sweatshirt under his red robe, and held Mark's service revolver, which he handed to Lane before speaking.

"I agree with Rusty, Jed," he said. "We'll stand up to the authorities with you all the way legally, but nothing illegal or dangerous can happen here tonight. No way."

The other Satanists nodded. Jed slumped in his desk chair. Lane used Rusty's cell phone to call the HPD substation. Jed reluctantly surrendered the .22 rifle. The fifteen minutes before the police arrived were tense. Finally, several patrol officers, a detective, and Sergeant Jones arrived.

Tom accompanied the female patrol officer who drove Will to the Marshalls' home, where Mary Powers anxiously waited. Will was silent during the car ride.

Tom briefly summarized the night's events to Mary and her parents. He stressed the importance of Will's attendance at his next appointment, and requested Mary call Sister Andrea to make an appointment for herself and Jed. An invitation to Jed was important, even if he refused.

When Tom returned to his townhouse exhausted, he called Andrea to summarize the ill-fated club meeting.

All the club members except Jed agreed to be interviewed without their lawyers, to avoid being taken to the police station. All said they had nothing to hide.

The officers and detectives took each of the men to separate rooms for detailed questioning about the evening's events. Each would have a copy of the completed police report to show their lawyers.

Sergeant Jones questioned a glum Jed Powers, who called a lawyer quickly to the scene. Jones questioned Jed with the lawyer present, and he carefully searched the room while the two men watched vigilantly. Jones placed a dead rabbit and a container of blood in a labeled evidence bag. An officer took careful photos of the club room, breezeway, and backyard. Lane's camera was retrieved from the bushes, and the pictures were secured as evidence.

All the men, including Jed, were let free on their own recognizance and scheduled for follow-up questioning appointments at HPD.

The club members left promptly with no words of good-bye. Jed sat at his desk in the club room, staring at the appointment card for his meeting with Captain Smith that Mark Lane gave him. A scowl filled his face. He needed a beer, preferably more than one. Though he still wore his robe, it was wrinkled.

CHAPTER 13

Therapy Begins in Earnest

Will arrived at his next appointment accompanied by his grandfather. Tom really liked Harry Marshall. His love and affection for his grandson was readily apparent in his glances at the boy. Harry picked up a magazine to read in the waiting area, as Will and Tom entered Tom's office.

Will plopped into a chair, scowling. He glowered at Tom for at least ten minutes. Between angry glares at Tom, he often stared at an empty chair across the room.

"You stupid, fucking, asshole, shrink doctor!" Will said. "I hate you!"

Tom leaned toward him and said softy but resolutely, "I don't want you to talk to me that way. I know you're angry, but inside I think you're scared and sad—mostly sad."

Will looked at the chair across the room, smirked, winked, and mouthed a few words Tom couldn't hear. Suddenly, Will leaped up and threw a punch at Tom's nose. Tom blocked it, grabbed Will, and wrapped his arms around him in a combination of a bear hug and a hammerlock, a hold he used occasionally with acutely aggressive, psychotic kids in the inpatient psych unit.

Will struggled briefly and stopped, but he remained tense, saying, "You gonna abuse me, shrink? Hurt me bad? I'll yell for my grandpa. See what shrinks do, Jake."

He used a goading, provocative tone, and his final phrase was directed at the empty chair across the room.

Tom said, "Will, I'd never hurt you, but I have to help you put your hate, anger, and other feelings into words. We must get that to happen. All human beings are helped by being able to talk out our feelings to someone we trust. It lets out the feelings that are blocked, puffed up, and ready to explode. That can prevent someone from being killed, hurt, or going crazy."

Will slipped back into his chair, glaring at Tom but looking slightly less angry. He seemed startled and even slightly curious, saying, "How do you know that can really do any good?"

Tom said quietly, "You know how much it helped to bitch to your friend Jake over there a minute ago? Most of us feel better when we have a good buddy to bitch to or share stuff with."

Will suddenly relaxed and turned toward Tom, asking, "Do you see Jake?"

Tom gently said, "I know he's there. By the sound of your words, I could tell he's your good buddy."

Will's dark eyes softened slightly. Will said, "Me or my dad could've shot you and that cop Saturday night. You shouldn't have been there."

Tom thought for a moment, then said, "Will, we figured the only way to stop the bad things your dad was doing was to get definite evidence for Judge Hartwell. We did detective work, like you did when you saw what your dad and his club members did to Brownie. Judge Hartwell, who gave us that search warrant, agreed. The other members of the Last Saturday Night Club agreed that killing or hurting anyone would be wrong. Sister Andrea and I tried to get your dad to come and talk about you, your family, and himself several times. So far, he won't do that to help you or himself, but I'm hoping he will."

Will looked sad, saying, "Does my father have to go to jail? I saw him hurt Brownie."

Tom said, "Will, I don't know. Only the judge and the court can decide that. More important is for your father to find a way to stop hurting your mind, your pets, and maybe other animals."

Will looked at the office clock, saying, "Ain't our time up? I got to go."

Tom said, "I'll see you next session." Tom held the door open for Will. The angry glare was gone.

Will's therapy had finally begun in earnest.

* * * * * * *

Jed Powers was still angry and resentful several hours after his follow-up interview with Captain Smith of the HPD. He cursed aloud about Smith, Lane, Tolman, and the other cops, and those uppity women like Jill Saunders of the DCYF and that bitch nun Sister Andrea. How did Will stand those wimpy sisters and queer fathers at St. Thomas More School all day? Jed planned to have his lawyer check, in careful detail, the Texas laws about child and animal abuse Captain Smith insisted Jed and his Satanist group violated. Four beers hadn't calmed Jed, but at least he felt a little sleepy.

Jed stopped pacing his castle room and took one more walk around the empty house. It was dark, and he was hungry. In the refrigerator, he discovered neatly prepared, wrapped sandwiches Mary left for the last club meeting, and wolfed down two. Did he miss Mary? He hadn't thought about her until seeing the sandwiches. They hadn't had sex in a year. It was longer since he felt warmth or affection from her. Mary became progressively more passive, quiet, and religious in recent years, probably because of her damn parents and that St. Thomas More joint. She was easier to control, but he hated her for fearing him. Jed wanted to be obeyed and respected, not feared.

Deep down, most men despised a woman who feared and cowered. The shrink would say Jed got what he asked for. *Screw the shrinks,* he thought.

He missed Will, though, and felt a twinge of sadness or loneliness, or maybe it was shame or guilt. It was hard to tell the difference lately. It was a shame Will saw his pet rabbit hurt. Will was a smart kid, but he needed to be older before he could fully understand the beauty of Satanic rituals. Jed hadn't known the damn rabbit was Brownie. He should've checked more carefully, but he was short of time before the men arrived. They became like his blood brothers that past year.

Jed thought about the fear and loathing he felt toward his dead father, Val. After Val died, Jed vaguely remembered promising to be closer to Will. When Will was little, they were close. They enjoyed trips to the library together and working on the rabbit hutch. Will even occasionally came to work with Jed on Saturdays. After Jed's plans for vet school fell through, things changed. His hope for a better life began to fade, bit by bit.

Jed drank another beer and sat on his bed. After the fifth beer, he slowly drifted off to sleep.

Suddenly, Val Powers loomed large over Jed's bed. Purple mist swirled about Val's snarling face. His teeth were yellow, and his breath smelled foul. His face was pale. His white hair was matted and greasy. Neck veins stood out dark purple. Jed tried to move but found he was paralyzed from the neck down.

Sweat poured down his face. As Val's soliloquy proceeded, his harsh voice sounded like an old, worn-out public-address system. When he spoke, puffs of purple mist spewed onto Jed and swirled around him. Val held a worn leather Bible in his right hand and pointed at it several times for emphasis.

Val said, "To say you're a disappointment, Jedediah, is a laughable understatement. You and your Satan crowd disgust me. Torturing little animals, starting fires in our backyard, and pissing in your bed as a kid was bad enough, but now you do it as a grown man. You think you're some big shot Satanic priest. That's nonsense. Mend your ways fast, before you lose everything, you loser!"

Jed still couldn't move, even when he saw Val's thick leather belt, with its thick steel buckle and steel studs down its length, snake through the purple mist toward Jed's exposed butt. Jed tried to scream, but no words came. His helplessness made the pain worse.

Jed, waking in a cold sweat, found he had peed in the bed, and there was vomit on the pillow. He shivered, recalling the nightmare. God, how he hated his father.

It was four o'clock in the morning. He stripped the bed and put the sheets and pillowcase in the washer. He showered, shaved, and dressed for work, settling for black coffee instead of a tempting beer.

He sat at the kitchen table to stare at the cards from Captain Smith and Dr. Tolman. Could a psychiatrist really help a guy understand a nightmare? Help nightmares go away? Could talking about it make it worse? Would the nightmares become more frequent?

Jed arrived at the Baylor Med animal resource center at eight o'clock. He looked forward to working with the animals and his coworkers for once. He thought of calling Mary, then thought about calling Tolman.

That brought a sardonic chuckle. How long had it been since he laughed? He begrudgingly admitted Tolman and Lane were gutsy and fair last Saturday. He fought acknowledging that inside, but damn it, it was true. That wasn't normal for damn Catholics.

Tolman said something else that was very important to Jed. Tolman spoke firmly but respectfully about Jed and his group's freedom of speech and worship. Could the Last Saturday Night Club move forward without animal sacrifices? The thought shook him. Rusty and the others expressed gratitude and respect to Jed despite the high anxiety of Saturday night.

Tolman seemed sincere in wanting to help Will. Maybe, just maybe....

Jed felt his eyes watering. He had a headache. His damn allergies must be acting up again.

CHAPTER 14

No Easy Textbook Answers

Sister Andrea made coffee for herself and Tom. She brought some of Tom's favorite doughnuts from Jerry's Donut Shop and chuckled , muttering to herself, "Sister, you're behaving like a contented wife."

Tom looked drained but happy to see her. They hugged, and he greatly appreciated the coffee and donuts.

"I was surprised to see that Jed Powers left a message for me," Tom said, "saying he would bring Will to his appointment on Thursday. Jed tried to cancel Tuesday's session, because he and the other Satanists are meeting with Judge Hartwell in his chambers that day. Jed said he wanted time to talk to me himself. I called him back and said I could talk to him at the end of Will's session on Thursday, but I expected Will to see me as usual on Tuesday. Jed wasn't pleased with that, but he agreed to see me Thursday."

"Wow," Andrea said. "Every so often, I love God's wonderful, prayer-answering surprises. That's a big bonus to the message I received that Mary Powers made an appointment to see me this week. I have to believe that the strong but kind way you and Mark Lane proceeded with those Satanists was a positive factor."

Tom said, "Andrea, all this good news scares the hell out of me. You know my Freudian, dark-cloud-hovering-above phobia. There's a vexing issue here. Just as I appear to be making baby steps of progress with Will, his Satanic daddy comes to the rescue. Or does he want to *be* rescued? I suspect, if Jed's seeking treatment for himself, he might not agree to see anyone but me. This might be the only window of opportunity to engage Jed in treatment. If I see him, will Will feel co-opted by Jed or think his own therapy is tainted? I've leveled some stout criticism of Jed and his fathering. Will Will feel upstaged by Jed, the great leader of Satanic men? Is Jed using the meeting to disrupt Will's treatment with me?"

Andrea's brow furrowed, as she became serious. He adored her sincerity and elegantly elemental beauty. She seemed an amalgam of the angelic, sexy, beautiful, and profound. He loved Andrea Albright and didn't feel the need to apologize to anyone for it.

"You should see Will first and explain your dilemma," she said slowly. "Let Will say what he thinks about your hearing whatever his father has on his mind. But explain to Will that you're his therapist. Tell him you'll try to get his father to see another therapist, someone you recommend and trust. I'd tell Will that you want him to be in the room when you hear what his father has to say. Remind Will that you once revealed his secret, but only because you felt someone was in danger. Will must know everything you tell his father that relates to Will. By the way, Dr. Rob Blanco would be good for Jed. He's good with meds if they become necessary, and he also does good work with men who have alcohol problems. Blanco is a steady, effective psychotherapist. He also is a loyal member of our Sacred Seven group."

Tom loved the way Andrea's mind worked. Andrea cogently explicated the key boundaries of the treatment relationships. She hadn't neglected the intensely important emotions pervading the situation, either. Rob Blanco was the same therapist Tom wanted to recommend to Jed. *Convergence of great minds*, he thought with a chuckle. Tom had been a colleague of Blanco's during his residency training in psychiatry, and they gave each other valued peer feedback and supervision over the years.

Andrea would be available to see Mary Powers alone, and when family sessions became necessary and possible, Mary with Jed. Those were their best-laid plans.

It was time for some of Jerry's best donuts and good coffee.

CHAPTER 15

Enter Authentic Justice

Will Powers was mad, sad, and a little frightened. He was mad because Jake sat so quietly in the rocking chair in Will's bedroom. Jake liked to stare at Will's large picture of a raven that hung over the head of the bed. Jake didn't seem to notice the raven. Will picked up the rabbit's foot that sat on his study desk. His father gave it to him for his birthday several years earlier and said it would bring good luck for Will and his rabbits.

Will stroked the soft fur and said, "Jake, I'm all mixed up about my dad and our Last Saturday Night Club. My feelings are jumbled up, because even the men didn't like what dad did to Brownie. They always respected my dad and his leadership. They went along with the ritual, but they changed their minds in front of the shrink and the cop. What do you say?"

Jake finally stared at the raven but said nothing. He always said he liked the bird's sharp beak.

"Come on, Jake. Are you changing your mind about the club, too? Say something, damn it!"

Jake mumbled, "Maybe you and the Satan club can just talk about the rituals and not actually have to do 'em."

Will threw the rabbit's foot to the floor, saying, "Now you piss me off! Lately, Dr. Tolman seems like a better friend than you. He pisses me off, but at least he listens carefully and says what he thinks and feels. If we just talked about the Satan rituals and didn't do them, that would be no fun. It would be like just talking about enjoying an ice cream cone or looking at a picture of one. I was looking forward to my six years being up, so I could be a full member of dad's club. Get out of my room. Go think over that stupid, pissant idea of yours!"

Jake teared up, left the bedroom, and slammed the door. Because Jake left, Will could cry. He picked up the rabbit's foot and imagined Brownie's soft coat and cute, wet, twitchy nose. He thought of his mother's warmth from a long time ago. She always bought veggies for the rabbits. He tried to push those mental pictures away, but some flooded back, especially those of dad with his red robe, gold belt, and gold dagger. The worst image was of dad's frightening face and cold, fish eyes.

Will put his face down on the bed. Tears washed away most of the scary pictures. The rabbit's foot helped, but Will was torn between pressing it against his face or throwing it at Jake's empty chair.

* * * * * * *

Judge John Hartwell was six feet two. Even at sixty years old, anyone would believe he played football and baseball at the University of Texas. He had gray hair and a suntanned, chiseled face that Jed felt resembled Dick Tracy or Spencer Tracy. In his black robe, Hartwell looked like a no-nonsense man. Jed suddenly thought about his dead father. Judge Hartwell had a look of power and authority, but without Val Powers's vicious anger. Thankfully, Val was dead and buried.

The Satanist club members stood facing the judge in his courtroom. All wore neat shirts with collars, and some wore ties. The scene was very different from the circle of chairs in Jed's castle room. The men seemed naked without their hooded red robes and black sash belts. Jed had no gold belt or dagger and stood like the others in the line of lawyered-up men.

Mark Lane, Sergeant Jones, Captain Smith, Tom Tolman, and several police officers sat to watch the proceedings. Judge Hartwell had interviewed Will Powers at length the previous day. Hartwell agreed with Tom Tolman's recommendation that Will be in the courtroom for the proceedings, though he would not ordinarily have allowed a twelve year old. He clearly saw the premature adult in the boy that Tolman had described. There was good news and bad news concerning Will. Hartwell knew that overly serious kids often became stars in their community in adulthood, but he also saw such kids turn into men like Charlie Manson or Willie Sutton.

Will sat quietly between his mother and Sister Andrea. Jed frowned at seeing the nun, but she stared steadily at him until he looked away. Several tense wives of the Satan club members were in the room, too. One dabbed her eyes with Kleenex. The court reporter was poised and ready to begin her work. No one smiled.

Hartwell, speaking calmly, was clearly in command.

"Gentlemen, your group's religious practice is unusual, but our country takes the First Amendment to the Constitution very seriously. I won't venture into the legal technicalities involved in the definitions of religious practice as it relates to your group. That topic has taken a complicated and sometimes-ambiguous route all the way to the Supreme Court. You and your lawyers can read the details of cases like *Church of Lukumi Babalu Aye v. City of Hialeah*, 508 US 520 (1993). The Supreme Court has allowed some statutes that criminalize religious conduct involving, for instance, ingesting poison or ceremonies with poisonous snakes.

"Aside from the legality of your religious practice itself, however, I conclude that in the course of your Satanic rituals and practices, you have violated two areas of Texas law. Sections 261.001, 261.101, 261.201, 261.103, 261.401, 261.405, and 260.407, as well as all of Section 261.000 of the Texas Family Code, provide clear definitions of child abuse, child neglect, and their various domains of investigation. When Will Powers was exposed to cruelty to his pet rabbit as part of a ritual at your meeting, it caused psychological pain and suffering to young Will. That was psychological abuse. It was also neglectful as a parent on the part of Jed Powers. An important mitigating factor in your case is that neither you members nor your leader, Jed Powers, were aware of Will's witnessing the actual animal cruelty—which, by the way, is also a serious violation and misdemeanor. Another significant positive mitigating factor in your cases is that you and your lawyers were cooperative and forthcoming to the police officers in this case, and to me at our earlier pretrial meetings and hearings. I commend all of you for that. I also commend and thank Sister Andrea Albright, Dr. Tom Tolman, Ms. Jill Saunders of DCYF, and the police officers, for their helpfulness in providing information to my court.

"This is also a first offense for all of you, so I won't impose jail time at this juncture. My decision is to fine each member of the group $300 and Jed Powers $500. This money will be given to a Harris County animal shelter after court costs are paid.

"In addition, your group is to cease and desist from all animal sacrifices. I have instructed Captain Smith's department to make random visits to your meetings over the next year to ensure this instruction is adhered to meticulously. I also caution all of you that even written descriptions about animal or human sacrifice in front of minors and highly sensitive adults can be traumatic. Men, don't violate my court order in that regard.

"Finally, I understand that Will Powers is in psychotherapeutic treatment with Dr. Tom Tolman, and that Jed Powers is prepared to seek consultation about treatment for himself. In addition, family and couples therapy for the Powerses is available through Sister Andrea at St. Thomas. She is well-trained and credentialed for such work. The special fund at St. Thomas will help the Powerses defray some treatment expense. If any of you other Satan club members or your families need treatment, my court has a list of well-trained professionals on whom you can call for assessment or treatment. I do not make these recommendations to you men and your families lightly, gentlemen. From earlier discussions, I take it that all of you will accept my verdict. Is that correct?"

No objections were made. They paid the fines, and court was adjourned.

As they walked out, Mark Lane said to Tom Tolman, "I wish justice occurred so swiftly and clearly more often."

Will Powers sat tense and attentive between Sister Andrea and Mary Powers during Judge Hartwell's statements, sometimes looking toward the empty end of the courtroom bench on which they sat.

CHAPTER 16

Son and Father

Will arrived at his therapy session exactly on time. Tom learned later that Sister Mary Agnes hadn't needed to remind Will to walk from his classroom to Tom's office. Jed arrived before his son, having promised Will he'd meet him at the office.

When Tom opened the door, Jed stood and started to walk through, but Tom stopped him in the doorway, saying, "Mr. Powers, Will and I are scheduled for this session. After we talk, you can have the time you requested."

Jed frowned, surprised, but he grabbed a magazine and sat down to wait.

After Tom and Will entered the office, Will took his usual chair. One of their peculiarly comfortable silences occurred. Tom chose to end it.

"Will, I hope your father told you he wanted to speak with me today. He probably has important things on his mind, but I wanted to talk to you and hear your thoughts first. I wanted you to know I'm *your* therapy doctor. Your father really needs therapy, but it can't be with me, though I want to hear what's on his mind. The therapy doctor I want to recommend to your dad is a man I respect and trust. If I agree to speak with your father this morning, I want you with us when we talk. What are your thoughts on that, Will?"

Will displayed his usual visage, a blend of an angry scowl and suspicion, though his usual paranoia seemed more like curiosity. Will said, "My dad told me he was going to be here. If my father says okay, that's good with me."

Tom asked, "Did your dad tell you what he wanted to talk with me about?"

Will shook his head and said, "Dad and I haven't been talking since that judge gave us his speech. That judge was mean to our club and especially to my father. Dad talked a little with my mom last night, but I couldn't hear what they said. They seemed a little friendlier. I think dad might tell you off today and stop this stupid therapy stuff. Let's get the talking with my dad over with."

Tom said, "Judge Hartwell wasn't being mean or unfair to the Last Saturday Night Club. It's his job to enforce the laws of the State of Texas. He did that honestly and fairly."

Will frowned without speaking.

Tom opened the door and shook hands with Jed as he entered the office. Jed glanced at the bookshelves before sitting in a chair beside Will.

"What's on your mind, Mr. Powers?" Tom asked.

Jed twisted his baseball cap in his hands for a moment. The cap and his uniform shirt pocket had the words *Baylor Animal Resources* printed on them.

"Doctor, I was prepared to tell you off good and proper after that court session the other day," Jed said slowly, "but I got to talk to you about terrible dreams I'm having, a nightmare. When I woke up I was drenched with sweat, and I saw that I had puked on my pillow and peed in my bed. In the dream, my dead father threatened me and said horrible things about me. It wasn't the first time I had a dream like that in recent months. They're getting more frequent. I heard from a guy at work and read in magazines that you psychiatrists can help a person who suffers from nightmares. It embarrasses me to talk about this in front of Will, but I think he's strong enough to take it. It might also help him."

Jed described his dream in detail. Will watched his father intently, clenching his fists more than once. He scowled when his dad mentioned he peed his bed, but he didn't speak. He glanced at the empty chair across the room several times.

Tom said, "Exploring dreams is one way we therapists try to help a person understand his unconscious mind, and the fears and conflicts that can constrict his freedom and harm his happiness. The person himself does most of the work in therapy, but the therapist helps. Sometimes therapy is painful and frustrating, but often it's like fascinating detective work. We all have vivid detective mysteries and treasures of insight hidden in our minds."

Jed's expression became tense while saying, "That court decision and my nightmare got me doing some serious thinking. I need help. For a long time, I haven't been a good father or husband. I seem all filled with anger, and my only safety valve is our Satan club. I won't give that up, but I want help. I hated you and Detective Lane at first, but I have come to respect both of you for trying to help. The legal confrontation hurt my wallet and my pride, but that damn Judge Hartwell was tough but fair. As a result, I know I want help. Will you see me in therapy?"

Tom was ready for that minefield, saying, "Jed, what you just said took courage, and I'm glad Will could hear you admit you need help. However, I'm Will's doctor, so I can't be yours, too. I want to recommend Dr. Rob Blanco. He has offices at the Hermann Professional Building in the Texas Medical Center. I trust and respect him, and I know he could be helpful to you."

Will stared at his father with an expression Tom found difficult to read. Those ever-present flashes of anger mingled with sadness in his eyes. Seeing the sadness gave Tom hope.

"I got to get help," Jed said. "I suppose I could see that doctor before or after work or on my lunch hour. I'll call him."

Will scooted quickly from the office and headed for his classroom. Jed lingered briefly and flashed a tight, brief smile, saying, "It means a lot to me that St. Thomas's special fund will help Mary and me pay for the 70 percent of the cost of our treatment that's not covered by our insurance. That ain't phony or hypocritical."

He donned his cap and left. As he often did after an important session, Tom sat engrossed in thoughts and swarms of feelings. His post-session reveries often revealed important hints about where the therapy was heading or where it might be stuck. He felt a surge of cautious hope and optimism, as if he were glimpsing a clearing ahead through thick forest and burned-out brush piles. Tom wondered, *What rare and elusive rewards are found in this damn impossible profession?*

CHAPTER 17

Sacred Group Supervision

Sister Andrea met Tom for coffee three weeks later. She reported that Sister Mary Agnes and Will's other teachers described a small but significant shift in Will's behavior. He smiled occasionally and participated in class activities more readily, even in Father Matthew's religion class. Will responded to questions with answers accurate to the textbook material or class notes, not from his repertoire of sardonic, cynical comments. Will became friendly with a boy and a girl in his history-study group.

Mary and Jed Powers saw Andrea for two couple's sessions. The first was difficult, because Mary was so passive. Then, with Andrea's firm but kind prodding and needling, Mary grew more vocal in the second session. Jed seemed sincere but was alexithymic and out of touch with his feelings. The couple's long journey of the process of naming feelings had finally begun. Andrea was pleased and so was Tom, especially about the fact that Jed and Mary's therapy wasn't progressing too quickly.

Andrea called Rob Blanco, but, because of privacy issues, Rob could say only that Jed was attending sessions regularly. Tom guessed that in Jed's early sessions a lot of anger was uncovered. He knew that Rob would take a lot of time before approaching Jed's angry-father dream, if Jed had even mentioned it. The timing and framing of a therapist's interpretations of stored rage at father figures was best done gradually and carefully. Rapport and trust between therapist and patient must be strong enough to weather the savage fierceness under the surface of someone who was abused or demeaned by a parent.

The strong tendency of such a patient was to transfer the rage to the therapist, who paradoxically seemed safer to attack. Blanco must be receptive to hear about Jed's rage, but strong enough not to become victimized by it. Tom recalled Will's attempt to punch him at an earlier session and remembered the stark graffiti, *Stupid*, written on the rear window of his beloved Silver B. Tom chose to remain silent with Will at this point.

For the first few sessions after the son-father session, Will was sullen and bristly. Tom let him vent lots of anger, which, not surprisingly, wasn't leveled only at Tom but at his father, too. He listened patiently to Will's angry words at Tom and Jed. At one point, Tom asked, "Do you think your father is still seeing Dr. Blanco?"

"Yeah, dad still sees that other damn head doctor!" Will snapped. His angry tone was a positive indicator reflecting Will's relief that his dad might keep getting help.

Tom thought, *It's amazing how paradoxes dance with surprising insights when good therapy occurs.*

Still, he had to be careful. He'd been wrong about apparently good sessions with Will in the past. Effective psychotherapy contained very few dramatic, emotionally charged, "Ah-hah!" sessions laden with insight. More often, there were several baby steps forward followed by an equal number of steps or slides backward.

The overall, long-term journey would hopefully be beneficial, but there were no guarantees. At the core of a successful treatment was invariably a deepening trust in the therapeutic relationship, as the patient frequently tested the therapist.

During Will's psychotherapy sessions over the coming months, he slowly but steadily appeared less angry and began to act a little more like a twelve-year-old kid. He wasn't Mr. Super Serious Pseudo Adult all the time. Tom and Will often played chess, which Will quickly learned to play well. Recently, he had been winning one-third of their games and showed signs of becoming a good loser, too. Ultimately, the success of any psychotherapy depended primarily on how solid the emotional trust and connection was between therapist and patient. Signs of a successful therapeutic bond were the emergence of the capacity for humor, challenging sarcasm from the patient, and the capacity to form friendships outside of therapy sessions.

During puppet play sessions, Will seemed to enjoy being the puppet master. Tom pretended to be one of Will's students who questioned his authority. Will made serious efforts to dominate Tom through sheer willpower and bullying, but they were unsuccessful. When Tom argued back and became irreverent toward Will, as the teacher, they laughed together. In their imagined classroom, Will laughed out loud when he said he'd make Tom stay after school because of disrespectful behavior.

Some of the more-interesting sessions for Tom were more serious and focused on death, how the body died, and some of the scientific studies of near-death experiences. Will entered those realms with serious study of the assignments Tom gave. He challenged Tom with lively questions that were phrased with less of a sardonic, bitter edge and more with challenging curiosity. Will, who could read well beyond the twelfth-grade level, became particularly energized as he and Tom read and discussed Dr. David Turell's brilliant, beautifully researched book, *Science vs. Religion: The 500-Year War: Finding God in the Heat of the Battle*.

The gripping descriptions and discussion about near-death experiences stirred many atheist arguments from Will. St. Thomas Aquinas would have been proud of how often those arguments tended toward soft agnosticism or even a dawning respect for the Christian and theistic viewpoint. Tom wished the Turell book had become a bestseller.

****

Penny Paulsen was a little younger than Will Powers. Though she was an inch shorter, she could run faster. Sometimes, she beat him in bicycle races, too. Secretly, Will always admired Penny for standing up to him in the schoolyard a long time ago when he had scared the little kids. Will was sorry he had hurt her with that pencil stab. He was very glad he hadn't hurt her eye. Penny had pretty eyes. During history and science club, Penny showed she knew as much as Will. At first, that made him nervous and a little angry. Her smile and funny giggle made it easier when she knew an answer he didn't. Somehow, that giggly smile reminded him of his pet rabbit, Whitey.

Penny had reddish-blonde hair and freckles. Other kids made

fun of her freckles, but Will secretly liked them. They reminded him of an old picture of his mom, who had freckles when she was a kid. Will hadn't told Jake, Dr. Tolman, or anyone else about his feelings for Penny. Sometimes, after a bike race, they drank water and talked as they rested. Will felt warm all over and blushed sometimes. Once, he kissed Penny, who giggled and clearly liked it. Will knew that she liked it, because she challenged him to another race. Penny even joked about Will's poking her near her eye a year ago. They both remembered her bleeding from Will's sharp pencil stab. Penny had gone to the school nurse for attention. Will now realized that he really liked her braveness. He told Penny finally that he was sorry he hurt her.

Penny was a nice mind picture for him. Will thought about her a lot.

* * * * * * *

Toward the end of the second year of Will's treatment, he asked Tom if he could attend therapy only once per week. He explained that he and his mother had started a newspaper delivery route to save money for Will's college fund and possible family vacations.

Jed Powers had received a promotion at work and asked Will to help him care for the Baylor lab animals two afternoons each week. Will had also become interested in St. Thomas More's science club, which participated in competitions with other parochial schools in the Houston area. Will frequently sat beside Penny during that club, and he recently invited her to the eighth-grade dance.

After Will presented his case well, Tom agreed to reduce their therapy session to once a week. In his heart, he felt the sweet sadness a parent feels when a child begins to grow up and away.

Their sessions continued once weekly, and Will came prepared with questions about lots of relationships, especially why Penny was so stubborn and difficult to understand.

"Penny just doesn't agree with my ideas," Will said, "even when I present them clearly and scientifically. Sometimes, she says I'm too science-minded. Penny thinks I should read more poetry. She read me a mushy one over the phone last night that made me embarrassed. Here it is."

Night Love
The night delights in your beauty,
For it blends with her silent self.
The expanse from dark till dawn,
Sings a low haunting song
To Life's restless subconscious.
It is here we linger, you and I,
Before the day and its realness.
Your eyes have spoken Love,
Now only God and I remember.

"You remembered that by heart," Tom said. "Have you studied love poems at school?"

Will replied, "Yeah, a few by Shakespeare, but they weren't as mushy as the one last night. I get thinking about something that came up a lot when we argued about the stuff in Dr. Turrell's book. We decided we could stay friends even if we disagreed strongly. Penny said I didn't have to like the poetry she does, but I have to respect that she likes it. I tell her about a lot of important things, but I never tell her about the Last Saturday Night Club."

Will paused for a long time before asking, "Did I tell you what my father and I talked about recently? The Last Saturday Night Club meetings have slowly changed. Right after that judge speechified at us, the club members had angry lawyer discussions. Gradually, Dad started asking other members to give talks at the meetings. I thought he was getting weak from talking to Dr. Blanco so much, but the meetings stayed interesting. Even more interesting was the fact that one club member had the guts to talk about his Jewish faith. He told us about how in the Old Testament times, God ordered animal sacrifices at the temples. Rusty figured God changed His ways to have men worship differently in New Testament times. I liked that discussion and asked the club members if I could talk about some things from Dr. Turrell's book, especially those near-death experiences. They said it would be interesting and they would read the book. I felt proud inside."

* * * * * * *

Several months later, Tom told Sister Andrea about the decision to reduce the number of sessions with Will. She raised further questions about the decision, but, after hearing about the details of the discussion between Will and his dad and the events at the Last Saturday Night Club, she agreed with the decision.

As Andrea told Tom about her recent successful therapy session with Mary Powers, Tom wept, saying, "I feel like you and I are symbolic parents for Will. I love you, Andrea. I wish we had known each other decades earlier."

Andrea gave a simple prayer of gratitude that God had been such a helpful presence in the treatment of Will and his family. It had been difficult. No important psychotherapy was easy. Later while alone, Andrea told God that she loved Tom Tolman and was angry at Him for not allowing their paths to cross much earlier. She laughed and cried with God at her sheer irreverence. His silence seemed to indicate He understood.

CHAPTER 18

Sacred Seven Gets Personal

Tom Tolman, Rob Blanco, Andrea Albright, Diane Pattison, and Jack Baines had been members of their monthly peer-supervision group for twenty-five years. At first there were seven members, and though they lost two members years later they continued to call themselves The Sacred Seven or The Secret Seven.

Tom, Rob, and Jack had been psychiatry residents together at Baylor College of Medicine's Department of Psychiatry. Diane was a psychologist who met Andrea when Andrea did her psychiatric social work training fellowship at Baylor's Department of Psychiatry and Texas Children's Hospital.

Each month the group's host provided food and drinks, and the group often discussed a book or journal article. The most valued part of the group for each member was the ability to present any aspect of his psychotherapy work or personal life. They grew to treasure the candor, accurate empathy, confidentiality, and respectfulness each member extended to the colleague who was on focus. Discussions were often intensely personal. The usually labeled "Hot

Seat" in many intensive therapy groups could more accurately be called the "Tough Love Seat" at the Sacred Seven meetings.

After a few years of building trust, the members grew steadily closer for decades. Meetings were vivifying to their therapy work and psychological vitality. All looked forward to the meetings. It became more important to them than paying their malpractice premium or office rent on time.

This evening Rob Blanco immediately asked for time. He was a slender man, five feet seven inches tall, whose enjoyment of tennis and jogging in the Houston sun controlled his weight and gave him an attractive tan. His dark eyes flashed.

"Guys, I have two heavy items tonight," Rob announced.

"Go for it, big guy," Diane said. "I got my heavy hose on."

Rob had often asked the Sacred Seven for intense supervision and support about the tumultuous sessions he had with Jed Powers. Early on, the group feared for Blanco's safety. Jed had seemed to confuse violent dreams about his dead father Val with perceptions about Blanco at their therapy sessions. Blanco had weathered those storms much to Jed's benefit.

Blanco said to the group, "Jed Powers announced this morning that he received a special fellowship to study veterinary medicine in Los Angeles. His boss at Baylor recommended him, saying his work had vastly improved, along with his attitude. The fellowship begins in three months and will likely lead to a permanent job for Jed at the UCLA Med Center's Animal Resource Center. The position would boost the family income, and animal medicine is a field Jed has always wanted to work in. He surprised the hell out of me by saying he talked it over with his wife, Mary, his in-laws, and his son,

Will. Mary supports him, but Will was quiet."

Tom said, "Several months ago, Will asked to reduce the number of his sessions to once a week. He continues to do good work on early adolescent issues. How has Jed been doing?"

Rob's brow furrowed as he thought. "As you guys know, Jed's first year of therapy was a grueling combination of Solomon-like, patient listening and name-that-feeling work, while agilely dodging Jed's vicious arrows of projective identifications. By the way, Andrea, your work with Mary and the Powers couple was very important. The process here in our group allowed us to anticipate impending crises and prevent us from getting split apart by Jed's transference rage."

Rob continued, "After the first year, Jed asked for three sessions a week and started using the couch during therapy work. He said it helped not having to look at my ugly face, but you know how distorted that perception is."

All chuckled. In the Sacred Seven, Jack Baines was the most classically trained in psychoanalysis. He was always clean shaven, and, at five feet eleven inches tall, was handsome and impeccably dressed. The group threatened to have a pool party in the hot summer months, so they could see him without a dress shirt and bright tie. Jack was sensitive to issues of separation and loss, and he was very knowledgeable about separation disorders in children.

Jack said, "Tom, I'm sure, has noticed how much detail I ask for about his work with Will Powers. My sense of things at this time is that what's crucial is the good work Jed has done with you, Rob. You guys know my bias about how important the father-son bond is for boys Will's age. Like a good psychoanalyst, I naturally would prefer that Will, Jed, and the Powers couple have another year or two in therapy, but modern, mobile American life is what it is. Andrea, what do you sense about Mary's true feelings about the proposed move to LA?"

Andrea said, "I think Mary has claimed her inner strength effectively. At her most recent session, she was anticipating her sadness at leaving her relationship with me. She's confident that Jed's on a solid, positive track. Like you implied, Jed's ability to stay connected to Will is crucial. Jed needs to hear how important he is to his son. I was very relieved to hear about their recent conversations about the Satan group, which was a remarkable change in itself. Will and Jed are both stubborn. Perfunctory referrals, even to recommended therapists in LA, I think would be a mistake. Our termination work with each family member would best be directed at consolidating their strengths and stressing their ability to make use of therapy in the future, as each one intuits his or her own needs."

Diane, an expert on group-therapy processes, agreed with Andrea about the change in the group dynamics in the Satan group. Then Diane confronted Rob.

"Rob, you said you had two issues to bring up?" she asked.

"I'll save it for next month. Our time has been well spent, and it's getting late."

* * * * * *

Psychotherapy for Will, Jed, and Mary proceeded in lively, active fashion. Each therapist kept an active focus on the powerful emotions surrounding their rapidly approaching graduation from therapy. Jed seemed ready to take leadership during the move, and Mary was supportive and assertive. She insisted she and Will would look in LA for a small business comparable to the paper route they had successfully set up in Houston.

Will's sessions with Tom became more difficult after the news of the LA move was announced and plans were starting to be made. Jack Baines told Tom that he needed to be on the lookout for Will's possible final good-bye to Jake and premonitory grieving for his separation from Penny Paulsen. Such a separation could be volatile. Tom felt great gratitude toward Jack and the group. He needed confidence more than ever in his work with Will. Once again, before his sessions with Will, he felt neck, head, and stomach tension like old somatic companions returning for a visit.

Will surprised Tom when he asked to return to having two therapy sessions per week. He said he'd let his mother do the paper route. Tom insisted the current treatment plan worked well, and the talks Will had with his mother while delivering papers were important. Will seemed relieved by Tom's decision not to increase the number of sessions per week, and Tom's muscle tension in his neck, head, and stomach ceased.

CHAPTER 19

Ever More Sacred Seven

The Sacred Seven group time arrived. That month, the group met at Diane Pattison's elegant apartment at The Houstonian, with its beautiful view overlooking Memorial Park and Buffalo Bayou. The pizza and beer Diane served were part of her irreverent charm.

Rob Blanco leaped into the breach after barely finishing his first piece of pizza.

"Tom and Andrea, I have to confront both of you about something that's been rumbling in my preconscious mind for several months. Are you guys in love and having sex with each other?"

Even the august members of the Secret Seven Group grew hushed for a few seconds, until Andrea and Tom responded simultaneously.

"Well….uhh… love…we…"

Andrea finally said, "I love Tom as more than a friend and I wish my vows didn't prevent me from making love with him. We've kissed and hugged. You know how much we enjoy being with each other, laughing and working together."

Tom wasn't blushing when his turn to reply came.

"I love Andrea, and we've both spoken angry prayers to God for not letting our paths cross decades ago. God's silence has led me to believe He or She understands. We would never try to hide our love for each other from this group. Speaking for myself, I can only say that the last year of special friendship with Andrea has helped me move beyond professional burnout. I've grown quietly happier than ever before in my life. I haven't been hiding my love for her, but I certainly don't know what to do with it or where to go from here."

Diane shared, "You guys all know I'm content with Rolf. After each of our prior unworkable marriages, we hang in a contented limbo on the verge of happiness and the dreaded M-word. Right now, though, I envy you two and feel happy for both of you. Damn, Tom, have you asked Andrea to marry you?"

Before he could reply, Andrea said, "Diane, my wonderful friend, Tom has gently asked, but I have quickly disallowed his proposal on the basis of some clerical neurotic principle. I've asked him for a year of concentrated, prayerful decision making. That was several months ago, and I've grown confident that I love Tom in that 'love-of-a-lifetime' way. I don't fear and have never feared the church authorities. I also feel that God will always extend His love and grace to me. God loves me, even if I yield to those delicious hormones He or She blessed me with before I jump through the Catholic Church's administrative exit hoops. So far, my celibacy is tenuously intact. The final domain of difficulty for my prayer process is the dread of how my departure from the church would negatively influence the Catholic patients and families I've worked with over the years. You all know of the sacred domain of commitment to patients."

Rob interrupted. "Damn it, Andrea, I'll never forgive you if you bullshit yourself with that last neurotic gig! Tom and I were talking the other day about the folly of treating psychiatry and psychotherapy like some religious ordeal ritual. You show me a therapist who deifies dedication so much that he works fifty-plus hours a week and barely sees his wife, kids, or relatives, and I'll show you a person headed for divorce and loneliness. There's even the good word from Jesus about the poor and needy. It fits your bogus fear that your patients will suffer if you do what's good and beautiful for yourself."

Rob went to Diane's bookshelf and took down a Bible, thumbing to a passage and reading aloud. "Mary took a very expensive bottle of perfume and poured it on Jesus's feet. She wiped them with her hair, and the sweet smell of the perfume filled the house. A disciple named Judas Iscariot was there. He was the one who was going to betray Jesus, and he asked, 'Why wasn't this perfume sold for three hundred silver coins and the money given to the poor?' Judas didn't really care about the poor. He asked this, because he carried the moneybag and sometimes stole from it. Jesus replied, 'Leave her alone. She has kept this perfume for the day of my burial. You will always have the poor with you, but you won't always have me.' " [John 12:3-8]

The group was transfixed until Tom said, "Blanco, you sly fox. Talk about stealing a priest or nun's thunder and turning it back on her."

Rob pressed on. "Look, Tom and Andrea, I'm no Jesus, and this pizza party ain't no Last Supper, but we love you two. I'm not a good, mass- attending Catholic, but in this room I sense the true spirit of what the real Jesus was about. Andrea, I know the quality psychotherapy work you do. I assure you that most of your patients, past and present, can come to terms with your decision and would want you to find the love of your life. The poor ones, who can't accept your prayerful decision, can find another caring person to help them heal their neurotic wounds. Either way you choose, we will continue to love you and welcome your precious input into our lives and the group. Spill that perfume, Sister, and don't sit out the dance."

Andrea began crying tears over her joy of their friendship. Diane handed her some Kleenex. The group sat in comfortable silence for some time.

"Many times," Tom said, "during sessions with Will Powers, I feel especially comfortable during the silences. That's how I feel right now, and that's why I love this group."

"Thanks, Rob," Andrea said. "That offering was special." She got up from her stuffed chair to sit between Diane and Rob on the couch, hugging them both.

Diane said, "Andrea, I'm happy for you and Tom, whatever your final decision. I know that all groups, especially church groups, can get petty and vindictive. Any group struggles with envy and fear when a genuinely loving couple forms in its midst. The couple who is happy with their love stirs up the ambivalence of many group members. Some feel happy for the couple. Others must face their own marital relationship and its current state of happiness and contentment or lack of either one, or worse. Regardless, you can be assured of this group's affection and support."

Jack Baines cleared his throat.

"I don't know any scripture, prayers, or benedictions, but Freud once said, 'Psychoanalysis is founded on complete candor.' That's what I love about this group."

They ate the remaining pizza and drank beer as they decompressed from the beautiful yet draining intensity of that night's meeting. For all, work began the following morning at seven or eight o'clock.

CHAPTER 20

Good-bye Jake Old Pal, et al.

Will Powers was as angry as he'd been in a long time. Jake was fast asleep in the chair across the bedroom. Will punched his shoulder to wake him.

"Jake, I got to get to school soon and do my paper route this afternoon, so we got to talk right now. Get awake, pal!. In six weeks, I'm going to California. You can't go with me."

Jake didn't answer.

"You gonna say something? Stop wasting those tears down your cheeks. I'll be spending so much time writing to Penny and saving money to call her that I won't have time for us anymore. Besides, you need to get stronger and make your own friends, especially a girlfriend. They can be sweet, buddy. I know you don't like Penny, but you can find someone almost as smart and pretty. I got to say good-bye now for good, Jake. Think like a raven, buddy. Feel like one. You'll be all right."

Jake wiped his nose with his sleeve, and they shook hands. He looked at the raven picture above Will's bed one last time.

At least Jake hadn't left snot on Will's hand. Will knew that Jake's watery eyes weren't caused by allergies. Dad said both their allergies would be much better in California.

* * * * * * *

April 15, 2004

Tom saw Will walking slowly toward his campus office. Will waved to Penny and another classmate. He used to protest coming to therapy sessions, but he currently seemed to regard it as a source of celebrity among his peers. He even referred a couple friends to therapy with Andrea, or, through her, to Jack Baines.

Tom felt calm but sad before his final session with Will. Most such sessions with kids involved a mix of feelings. There was envy for the child's good years ahead, satisfaction and admiration for the child's growth, and pleasure over the successful, creative therapy work accomplished. Tom often felt like a gardener who watered, weeded, and fertilized while mostly staying out of the plant's way.

Will knocked and came in.

"Hey, head doctor, I talked with Penny about missing her like you said might be good. That was hard, but it didn't get as serious and tense as I thought. She listened and didn't cry or laugh. She said she'd miss me, too. She gave me some suntan lotion for California and a miniature surfboard with a rabbit's foot attached. I told her I'd call the rabbit Penny the Surfer Girl. She laughed that musical laugh I like, and I laughed with her. She thought writing once a week was good, because I write slower than her. She'll save money for phone calls, too. Her family might visit Disneyland, and then we could see each other. Dad said he'd take me with him when he comes back to Houston for conferences at Baylor. I'd like that. You know, dad seems stronger this year. I know he's happier, because I hear him and mom laughing when they wash dishes or watch TV together. Dad's doctor helped him a lot."

Will stood and walked toward the bookshelves.

"I'm glad you got Dr. Turell's book for the library. It's better than those dusty, old church history books. I still might write a book someday."

Tom asked, "What would you call it?"

Will thought for a minute.

"Today, I'd call it *Many Different Ideas about Death and Life*. Penny thinks I should call it *California Dreamin'*. That's an old song her parents like. They danced to it when they were in high school. I was going to give you a good-bye gift. I thought about getting you a shrunken head I saw in a store for fun, but instead I got you this book of poems, *Special Poems of 2004*. I know you like poetry. I wrote a poem for you on a blank page at the back of the book."

Will handed the book to Tom. It was wrapped in Christmas wrapping paper. After shaking Tom's hand, Will moved quickly to the door but paused before exiting, flashing his dark-eyed grin with eyes that radiated warmth. He gave another wave and dashed toward the classroom, though he moved more slowly than on the first occasion they met.

Tom opened the wrapping and turned to Will's poem at the end of the book.

My Doctor
Some doctors give shots and pills
Other doctors cut a lot and stitch
My head doctor heals my mind
By my finding words to cure ills.

CHAPTER 21

A Politically Incorrect Happy Ending

January 15, 2014

Even in mid-January, Houston was so hot and muggy that the AC in Tom and Andrea's apartment had to be turned to very cold. After he turned seventy-four, Tom began to enjoy late-afternoon naps on most of the four days a week he wasn't working. When he napped, he had the habit of wrapping himself in a sheet like a cocoon. It was wrapped so tightly, Tom couldn't escape when Andrea began her playful tickle attack. She took advantage of his helplessness as long as possible. Finally, Tom wrestled free and held her in his arms. A long, enthusiastic kiss was a nice contrast to being tickled.

The delightful fragrance of the perfume in her hair added to the intoxicating music of her giggles during the tickling. She twisted out of her soft sweat suit, and her adoring eyes added visual erotic hypnosis to the skin-to-skin delight of foreplay. Her breasts swelled in unison with his erection. The ensuing rhythms of lovemaking came to a crescendo and blended into a delightful, gentle love dance.

After their afternoon delight, they cuddled on the bed. Nothing compared to the afterglow of good lovemaking, particularly for happily married lovers. Tom cherished those moments of loving and being loved. He thanked God he found it before the exit angels whispered his name.

Mrs. Andrea Tolman smiled and said, "I'd love to stay here in our nest all evening, but we have only an hour to prepare to host the Sacred Seven Group. Fortunately, I bought drinks and salads earlier this afternoon. You can cook Domino's pizzas to perfection."

They showered together before their final preparations for their guests. As was often the case, Jack Baines was a bit early, so he and the Domino's pizza man arrived simultaneously. The others followed soon thereafter, and all began eating salad and pizza.

Diane Pattison wanted to discuss a new patient whose husband recently became involved in a group calling itself The New Light. She read Tom's book about destructive cults and wanted to hear Tom's thoughts about her patient. Jack would have some input regarding children in a family where the father was hooked by a cult.

Before they began the discussion, Rob said, "Guys, did you see the note about Will Powers and his family in the St. Thomas More Church bulletin? Jed Powers wrote a poignant letter addressed to the entire congregation, thanking them for their prayers and the financial help the church offered him and his family. The therapy they received, he said, saved their lives and souls.

The bulletin also announced that Will Powers won a faculty award at UCLA. Will's now an instructor of English literature. Will and a colleague from the communications department at UCLA wrote a book together about the use of poetry and poetry study groups to help communication and understanding between various ethnic, social, and religious student groups. The group described in the bulletin involved students from a large mosque in LA and Catholic students from the LA diocese. They meet each month to share poems and divide into small groups to read poetry and write a group poem. Over time, those group poems evolved into intimate themes that allow respect and understanding of each others' writing skills and religious beliefs. There was even a group of atheist students who saw how emotionally powerful their non-beliefs were as the dialogue developed with the Muslim students."

Andrea grasped Tom's hand. "That's great news, Rob! I believe the prayers of at least five people I know of had an impact on Will and his parents' treatments. There must've been a cumulative effect that led to exponentially positive effects on the power of God's presence in the fabric of Will and his parents' treatment."

Jack cleared his throat. "My Freudian form of incompetent atheism has been converted to insecure agnosticism, as I listened to discussions of the Powerses' treatments in this group. I was deeply impressed by the healing of Jed and Will Powers's attachment disorders, as they worked with Rob and Tom. Their active efforts to find words to describe, identify, and change bitter rage and painful isolation into creative activity was the cure. Hard work like that in therapy turns passive feelings of hurt, rage, and isolation or victimization into creative vocational, educational, and social experience. Tom, don't get a swelled head, but your patience with Will's bitter barrages was impressive. Rob, your tightrope walk with Jed's violent anger and raging paternal transference was equally successful. I'll always remember that session you described in detail, when Jed suddenly stood, towering above you with a beet-red face, poking his finger at your chest, and saying, 'Damn you, Val! I mean, Rob. My mind just went Blanco. I mean blank.' "

Jack heaped further praise. "During those slips of the tongue, I thought he might try to punch you. Instead, you stood, put your arm on his shoulder, and said, 'Jed, thank you for allowing me to substitute for Val Powers right here and now. From where he is right now, probably in purgatory somewhere, he damn well ought to be proud of your guts in facing the part of yourself that was dominated by Satanic Val Powers. Now you can truly say, 'Go to hell, Val,' and move on to be your own man and a good father to Will.' Jed was blown away when he realized that he actually saw Val's face superimposed on yours. He heard his father's voice over your own. Though dead for years, Val was present in that moment. Jed had a vivid experience with you. That flashback of transference, as we call it, was so real that it gave Jed deep conviction. The fear of Val's ghost blazed. The ability to overcome fear of the Val within was also an inner victory lap. Then you both marveled about Val's final, ugly visitation to your therapy session. Jed's sudden insight was saturated with here-and-now emotion, and lubricated with spontaneous tears. That kind of insight lasts a lifetime and isn't just intellectualized. It sticks to the ribs like good ole chicken-fried steak with mashed potatoes and gravy. Damn, but that's what good psychotherapy is all about! Rob, it's like I have a permanent videotape in my mind of that session. Now Jed helps and heals animals instead of cutting them up for Satanic sacrifices."

Rob reminded Jack that he and Jed had many quiet, consolidating sessions that were less dramatic but equally important, but another dramatic session did occur later during Jed's therapy when they went to Val Powers's gravesite. Jed asked Rob to accompany him there on the anniversary of Val's death. He hadn't attended Val's funeral and talked about pissing on his grave that day. Rob was prepared to witness that act, but instead the rainy day was punctuated by a stream of angry cuss words. Next came a flood of tears that Rob said were lubricating Jed's soul. They were symbolic of Jed's freedom from the Val within.

Both Jed and Rob were convinced that Jed would have no more nightmares about Val.

The Sacred Seven experienced a long silence that was pregnant with a collegial tone of reverence and a pleasant, playful sense of wonder. All shared respect for the victories of psychotherapy work and were painfully aware of its—and their own—limitations and defeats. Over the years the Sacred Seven members had done psychological autopsies after patients' suicides or homicides, and had always comforted each other. Thankfully they were not common.

The discussion about Diane's case seemed anticlimactic after the joyous news about Will, Jed, and Mary Powers. It was interesting in light of how far Diane's patient and her family had to go before they might have a chance for the same freedom that Jed obtained from Satanism.

After their guests left, Tom and Andrea held hands on their apartment's small porch and looked out over a gradually and pleasantly cooling Houston.

POSTSCRIPT

Although the man and his wife were both naked, they were not ashamed. [Genesis 2:25]

* * * * * * *

During Freud's heyday of fame, a reporter was said to have asked him, "How can a person find happiness?"

Freud said simply, "He or she must successfully learn how to love and to work."

Tom and Andrea Tolman would add, "And to work and be playful with friends."

* * * * * * *

Readers…Little did Andrea and Tom know that a huge new challenge will soon thoroughly test their skills.

COMING SOON by Peter Alan Olsson, MD—*Houston's Homegrown Terror* and *A Boy Who Loved Knives*

EXISTENTIAL ADDENDUM
A Dream of a Psychiatrist's Theology of Benevolent Revenge

Dr. Tom Tolman wasn't able to sleep on the night of September 12, 2001. He disobeyed one of the cardinal rules of sleep hygiene: He worked past midnight on his perpetually expanding manuscript about apocalyptic cult leaders. He began writing the book twenty-three years earlier after seeing the ghastly pictures of the bloated bodies of 918 men, women, and children near Jim Jones's jungle pulpit in Jonestown, Guyana, in 1978.

At 11:00 p.m., he suddenly realized that the 9/11 killer, Osama bin Laden, was the ultimate destructive cult leader. Bin Laden used recruitment techniques, distorted religious persuasion, and mind-control concepts similar to those used by Jim Jones, David Koresh, and other destructive, messianic cult leaders.

Tom had been studying those malignant pied pipers for two decades. Bin Laden's evilly applied Islamic theology was used to enliven his message of hatred toward the West, the US, and Western leaders, who seemed unaware of the power of Bin Laden's sinister applied theology. Many thousands more would die at the hands of Bin Laden's terror cult.

Osama appealed to the phase-specific rebellion of Muslim adolescents like a malignant, modern Muslim rock star or a Robin Hood. Tom knew that Osama would occupy an entire section of his book. His mind raced as he made notes and outlines about his observations of the man. He pictured Osama's smirking, perfidious smile and scraggly beard. Seeing that image made falling asleep a psychological project that night.

Humans can't will themselves to sleep. The final lowering of the curtain of sleep, though highly valued, is an afterthought, a surrender or pause in the stubborn, paradoxical, futile struggle to willfully become asleep. Tom tossed in bed and entered only the lightest levels of sleep until he finally arrived at the fuzzy threshold of deeper sleep.

He finally ceased his willfulness and eased into dream sleep, where he floated into a gigantic group-therapy room with amorphous gray walls and what seemed like an infinite number of leather chairs set in a large ellipse, with Tom in the leader's chair at one end. The optics of the situation were unique, in that he saw every individual in stark detail. Though they could hear him, they seemed unable to see him clearly.

A lively, emotional group process was going on, with anger the dominant feeling. Denial and fierce projection pervaded the group's psychology like a quiver of poisoned arrows readily available to each member.

To the left of the ellipse was an even larger area that contained countless smoldering, smoking piles of dead leaves. White, gray, and purple smoke floated endlessly around the horizon. Warm winds blew the mists about. Shadowy figures paced randomly in the foreground. Their frantic-sounding muttering was barely audible. Behind them burned some brighter fires, and screams of anguish rose occasionally, slightly muffled by distance.

To the right of the group-therapy area were lush, green fields; clear, pure streams and lakes; and distant, beautiful mountains that resembled the Swiss Alps. Nearby were happy people dressed in bright clothes, playing musical instruments, dancing, painting landscapes, and talking in small, animated groups, wearing bright smiles and occasionally exchanging spontaneous hugs. Citizens of that brighter horizon occasionally walked slowly near the edge of the group, carrying large placards with phrases like *Listen to each other, Listen to your inner soul, Forgiveness starts with inner truth-seeking, Guiltless ones throw stones first,* and *The soul of forgiveness is very patient but not patient forever.*

Tom's attention focused on the therapy group. A frowning, obese couple complained bitterly. The husband was pasty faced and of medium height, and spat words in rapid bursts while glaring at Tom.

"I don't know why my wife and I are in this place. What the hell's going on here, Doctor?"

"Mr. Brown, your folder indicates that you and your wife sexually and psychologically abused your daughter until her second-grade teacher turned you both in to child-protective services. The purpose of this group is for you two to confess your terrible behavior, so you can begin to seek forgiveness from your daughter, the heaven community, and, perhaps, yourselves."

As the wife frowned deeply, Mr. Brown snarled, "That's nonsense. That kid had a vivid imagination. She never showed us obedience and respect. Now you experts believe a kid's word over ours?"

"Mr. Brown, we believe your daughter. The medical report is conclusive. Your deaths by sudden heart attacks were merciful compared to your daughter's continued life of psychological suffering. However, you and your wife will be here as long as it takes to resolve your spiritual crimes to the satisfaction of the Great One."

Off to the left in the dimly lit, smoky haze, people implored in unison, "You two! Listen to the doctor and seek forgiveness."

The glaring Browns shouted insults at the helpers outside the circle. "Fuck off, you queers!" Mr. Brown said.

Tom noticed another couple nearby who'd been silent so far. "What are your names?"

"I'm Lynetta Jones, and this is James T. Jones. He don't talk too easily or much. You probably knew our son, the Reverend Jim Warren Jones, the famous leader of the Peoples Temple."

Tom said, "Infamous is a better word to describe your son, Mrs. Jones. I know a lot about him and both of you from reading newspapers, magazines, and books. Frankly, Mrs. Jones, I often wondered why you or your husband didn't notice the loneliness, anger, and gathering storm of evil in your son. You might have done something about it. Were you aware of how starved for empathy Jim was? Clearly, you and your husband neglected and thereby psychologically abused your son."

Lynetta Jones bristled. "My husband was beaten down after being traumatized by gas in World War I. I did my best to support us financially, Doctor. I encouraged little Jim not to be like his daddy. I told him to be somebody in life. He had to do it himself. I could tell he would become a great leader. In fact, I dreamed of him becoming like Albert Schweitzer."

Tom confronted Lynette firmly. "Mrs. Jones, your son led 918 people to a ghastly death in the Guyana jungle. Part of the reason for his terrible crime was the way you lived out your sick power dreams vicariously through your son. It didn't help that you put down his father in front of him, either. That made him seek to be the all-powerful father-God to his cult members."

Lynetta's eyes darkened. "Doctor, I was down there with the Temple people, and it was a paradise. The US government and meddling politicians were the real problem. That was true before we went to Guyana and after we arrived. My husband never saw our son's paradise in that country."

Billows of purple smoke erupted from her mouth while she spoke, while a tear ran down her husband's cheek.

Tom felt amazed.

"Mrs. Jones, face the truth. A year after you died, Jim grew more paranoid. He spent even more time preparing his Peoples Temple followers for group suicide."

She smirked, saying, "Lies, lies, and more lies. Regardless, it's better to die for a good cause."

Tom shook his head, saying softly, "You and James face a lot of hard psychological and spiritual work in this group."

The two glared at him while purple smoke drifted toward them. Tom looked at a new group, feeling exhausted when he saw how many were waiting in long lines outside the room—the waiting list of evil.

"Why are you looking at me?" a new woman asked. "Leave me alone. I ain't done nothin'. The warden with white hair said I had to come to these group meetings."

Tom's voice softened as he looked at the fearful, defiant teenage girl. "I'm Dr. Tolman, the leader of this group. What's your name?"

"Kathleen Maddox."

"Kathleen, your file indicates you abandoned your son, Charles Manson, when he was five years old. You neglected him before that."

"Doctor, how can you blame me for being a bad mother when they threw me in jail? Charlie stayed with his aunt and uncle while I was in prison. They're real religious people."

"You went to jail for armed robbery. Charlie was only five years old, Kathleen. He was confused and upset because you let him do anything he wanted, and suddenly you were in jail while he was in a strict religious home."

"As soon as I was paroled, Doc, I took Charlie away from his aunt and uncle and kept him with me. He was eight years old."

"Your file indicates you dragged him from one drunk boyfriend's house to another. Charlie soon ended up in a series of boys' schools and ran away from Father Flanagan's Boys Town. He eventually ended up in prison, and a psychiatrist there felt he was deeply ashamed of you. Charlie told reporters that jail was his real home. Eventually, he convinced several young women to brutally murder a beautiful, pregnant movie star named Sharon Tate and her unborn baby.

"Your Charlie got those women, who were approximately your age when he was born, to become murderers and spend the rest of their lives in jail. He created, romanced, and controlled jailbirds like you. People's unconscious minds use repetition, re-creation, and reenactment in the present in an attempt to undo the past or seek revenge for pain they experienced in the past."

Kindly people in white robes from the right side of the room asked Kathleen to accompany them to pray at the Room of Past and Future Forgiveness.

"Go to hell, you creeps!" Kathleen shouted.

The kindly people smiled. "We'll return again," they said in unison. "There's plenty of time to avoid doing hard time."

Tom felt exhausted in this endless dream, which contained smaller dreams that seemed like tributaries of the main river of spiritual emptiness.

Like a weightless astronaut, he floated into a nearby room labeled *Sacred Supervision*. He saw comfortable chairs, with three older, kindly people waiting and jotting notes into file folders. All the files had his name on the outside. The three people introduced themselves by their first names.

"I'm Wendy," one said. "Good start. Your directness was helpful to the group, Tom."

Tom said, "You say it was a good start, but those people are so filled with denial and anger that I feel they'll never change. I don't think there's enough empathy in all of heaven to help them."

In the distance, he heard a poem being read, with Dave Brubeck's *Take Five* as background music.

> "A view of Society's fragile existential glue
> Composed of hearts bound with love and hate,

We euphemistically call it family values.
They search my face in their vulnerability.
Fearing my words as if they were scalpels,
Anticipating pain of truths quite unwanted.
They struggle to prevent inevitable change,
By constructing coarse cobwebs of anger
They guard their feelings with steel walls
A masquerade of spurious protection
Merely composed of each others' strengths.
Family fears forming desperate projections,
Smothering freedom with trivial talking.
I must take risks with my inner family
To make an awkward contact with theirs.
Where do credentials come for this?
To attempt such a delicate journey together."

Abruptly, a tall, slender man with a long, white beard, who reminded Tom of his old therapist named Cal, appeared, and said, "Be patient, Tom. Forgiveness is a long process, not a glib statement. Cruelty, evil behavior, and the psychological suffering inflicted on children stems predominantly from self-absorption and a relentless obsession with an undoing or a utopian redoing of the abuser's childhood experiences.

"Utopian rescue efforts never work, because the would-be rescuer or savior ends up abusing or neglecting the child he thought he would rescue or save. The reminders of the original thorny garden of hate are too great. The formerly abused finds it too tempting to lord over, dominate, and hurt the more helpless child, as he was once hurt or neglected.

"Freud discussed *thanatos,* the death instinct. Deep within mankind's biology and our minds' collective unconscious are forces that magnify urges toward murder, suicide, and destruction. They often seem as if they were stronger than reason, conscience, and even science. The worst forms of *thanatos* are found in the relentless hubris of religious fundamentalists. God says that His earth project is often disappointing to Him. One reason is that the process of being a good person requires more than having a good education, loving parents, and attending a church, mosque, or synagogue. Spiritual salvation never results from simply believing the correct idea or practicing a correct ritual. Spiritual salvation or wholeness requires hard psychological and spiritual work. Like in physics, force over the distance of a lifetime equals work, and the ultimate test occurs when a man or woman becomes a parent. Allah, God, or Yahweh has a real intense thing about parenthood. He always remembers harm done to a child—without exception. You should see the shock, disappointment, fear, and outrage in Group D, where the radical, fundamentalist Muslim suicide and homicide bombers are confronted. They should have thought about their suicide bomb blasts many times over before they took children's lives.

"In Luke 18:15-18, Jesus said that one day some mothers brought their babies to him to touch and bless. But the disciples told them to go away. Then Jesus called the children over to him and said to the disciples, 'Let the little children come to me. Never send them away. For the Kingdom of God belongs to men who have hearts as trusting as these little children's. And anyone who doesn't have their kind of faith will never get within the Kingdom's gates.'

"Jesus went further in expressing God's final word, saying, 'And any of you who welcomes a little child like this because you are mine, is welcoming me and caring for me. But, if any of you causes one of these little ones who trusts in me to lose his faith, it would be better for you to have a rock tied to your neck and be thrown into the sea. [Matthew 18:5-6]

"It takes a long, long time for even a few of those suicide bombers to begin to realize the selfish, evil audacity of their homicides. Besides, they're becoming plentiful. Pakistan's madrassa schools alone produce one or two bombers per day. The schools also promote a narrow, spiritually destructive, fundamentalist mentality. They urge hate for anyone who believes differently.

"The mind God created in a child needs to be treated respectfully and gently, like a valuable, delicate flower. Narrow, rigid, judgmental teaching can pervert it. Sometimes it takes thousands of hours for our sad murder and suicide perpetrators to conduct interviews of the spouses, children, relatives, and friends of their victims. Finally, they recognize their evil, selfish acts for what they were.

"Sometimes, it takes Allah's actual scowling or frowning presence to convince murder bombers of their guilt. The earth literally and figuratively trembles when Allah frowns. Sometimes, black holes simultaneously explode in other galaxies. Only mystics and psychotic persons recognize God's message in earthquakes, hurricanes, tornadoes, forest fires, floods, and droughts. In each natural disaster, only God knows the infinite details of which came first, the human pain, suffering, genocide, and social injustice at a particular location, or the disaster's inherent pain, with its worldwide, blaring, and sensationalized TV coverage. Thus, TV captures the scenes and sounds of pain and suffering. TV sometimes seems like a new form of God's omnipresence. The seemingly serendipitous uncovering of social and political injustice on TV doesn't register in people's minds as causally connected.

"The recent earthquake in China poignantly revealed the discrepancy between the safety code expenditures required for business buildings compared to schools. God's tears and frowns roared and shook through the cosmos because of the thousands of dead children under the rubble. God's spirit wandered quietly among the grieving Chinese parents and grandparents.

"Likewise, Pakistan's quake, San Francisco's quake, and New Orleans's hurricane flood all reveal and conceal what God calls the essential creative products of His planetary emotion projects. Darfur in recent days had best be aware and beware."

Tom left the supervision area. In that amazing place, small groups sang, played music, and read poems. Music and poetry seemed the lifeblood of that dream place.

"Words can dance to music on pages, just like shoes on dance floors," a voice said.

Tom heard a poem being read in a stentorian voice to a small group on the porch outside the supervision room.

Tears Again at the Earth Project
In the infinite spaces between molecules
Where antichrists perform their dances,
God pauses to ponder, frown, and smile sadly.
His earth project is struggling to survive again.
Mankind's hapless, cyclical, grand rebellions

Power lust disguised as benevolent crusades.
Human clowns faithfully fail to reflect God.
And the sad, wonderful fools always forget.
Scientists try to measure the rippling strings.
Changes in energies so proudly measured,
So they can take pride in curiosity satisfied.
Atheists never brilliant enough for proofs.
Agnostics possess tiny flickers of humility.
Poets get sudden inspiration and compose,
With thankful hearts for Truth's reluctant gift.
Kierkegaard's leap of faith, still barely possible.
His patience tested, waiting for new Bethlehems.
Here my soul has found my faith in God again."

Cal smiled at the poetry reading and continued his lengthy, calm, and passionate soliloquy.

"Finally, Tom, the murder bombers begin to get Allah's message, and the long, scorching desert of their shame begins, as does our work here. As you can tell, time here is unusual. It doesn't follow the parameters of earthbound time, nor the constrictions of human thought and language. Newcomers are often shocked and humbled when exposed to glimpses of infinite varieties of moral compasses found in other places in God's universe. Space expeditions from Earth long after your lifetime there discovered myriad forms of God's personality and community group projects.

"The confounding variables fascinating even for the mind of God arise in how to combine and harmonize personal freedom with personal and group responsibility. Some evenings, Einstein and

Freud conduct group discussions on that topic and its corollaries. God is the *ex officio* leader of that group. Hubris haunts all the nooks and crannies of human history and the fabric of what we call human nature. The demon of religious minds is the fundamentalist mentality. It involves the endlessly smug conviction that one person or group has sure knowledge of everything that is good, evil, or the Truth. That's why rational argument, intellectual processes, and insight are such feeble tools in our work. The Great One has chosen these groups to accomplish here what so badly faltered at the earth project. Human groups have always had much power for good or evil. It's scary, Tom. Brutal, self-absorbed dictators, popes who ignored the horrors of predatory pedophilic priests, and martyrs for false causes are our most difficult clients. Joe Stalin, in purgatorial Group C, has spent many decades in his group. Recently, he seemed less paranoid and even nostalgic when his group leader got him to talk about his days in seminary before he joined Lenin's Bolsheviks. However, Stalin will probably soon face the Great One's personally presented ultimatum. Hitler, after many eons here, did. Adolph didn't even break down after a decade of cosmic art therapy group. Occasionally, we heard Adolph's cries for mercy from that distant lake of fire on the left. Adolf's anguished screams of pain are poignant. His endless pain is physical, psychological, and spiritual. Just as powerfully painful for him are the long periods where he's totally alone in the dark. He experiences exponential crescendos of pain in proportion to how much pain he brought others, particularly Jews.

"Tom, the true, final depth of hell is infinite loneliness. We've heard that Osama bin Laden was almost sent there recently. When he comes, he'll be in Group C. His father, Mohammed bin Laden, will soon be in your parents' group. Keep up the good work, Tom. It's time for you to return to Group M."

"What's the significance of that designation?" Tom asked.

Cal smiled. "Some staff thought it stood for Mothers' Group, or Parents' Group, but it means the Maybe Group, as in, 'Maybe the stubborn, psychologically ignorant, and self-absorbed can finally see God.' Atheists are the worst. They think they know more than they're capable of knowing." He smiled again. "Maybe your supervision time is over. Enough for now, Tom."

Cal reminded him of another person with the same name. Tom returned to the group feeling strangely refreshed. Several new members were in the group. A young couple sat several chairs apart but glanced frequently and fearfully at each other. Seconds felt like hours.

"What are you names?" Tom asked.

"I'm Bobby Howell," the man said. "I shouldn't be here."

"You sure as hell should be here, Bobby," the woman said. "You're Vernon's father."

"The group should know that their son, Vernon, was better known as David Koresh," Tom explained to the others. "He led eighty-five of his followers to a fiery death at Mt. Carmel in Waco, Texas, on April 19, 1993. Twenty-five of them were children."

"I was only fourteen years old when you got me pregnant, Bobby," Bonnie Clark said tearfully. "You never really loved me. You left us."

Tom said, "Mr. Howell, your file indicates you rarely saw your son in the years after you left. He told his cult followers years later, 'I was born only because my daddy felt something in his loins and lusted after my mama. There was no love there.' "

"Doc, looking back on it, Vernon was right," Bobby said. "Can't a man make a mistake?"

"Just because you don't love a woman and leave," Lynetta Jones said, "don't mean you didn't have responsibility to see your son and help raise him. By the way, Doctor, that is why I didn't leave my husband."

Howell glared at her, saying, "You uppity bitch! At least I made a clean break and didn't stay in a miserable situation. I gave me, Vernon, and Bonnie a clean slate. Vernon didn't like seeing me, anyway."

"Bobby," Tom pointed out, "many kids act that way for a long time after their parents split. They're testing the strength of their parents' love and sense of responsibility. You were fooling yourself."

"Doc, I want out of this group," Bobby Howell said. "It only makes me feel worse. Can't I do carpentry to work off my guilt time?"

"That's not how it works here, Mr. Howell. Just like a father-son relationship after a divorce, it often takes a long, long time to work out. Getting forgiveness processed here can take even longer. This group had better start working together. We'll take a short break now. The prayer room is always open. As you've learned, we never sleep here."

The group erupted in shrieks and curses through clenched teeth. Tom slipped into the empty supervision room for a break and shut the door. Coming into the room through another door was Sister Andrea, holding a small boy's hand. Will Powers's face glowed with an uncanny mixture of love, hate, and sadness. Sitting quietly in a corner was Joan, crying.

Tom welcomed his shrill alarm that morning. He awoke drenched in sweat, feeling totally drained. Tom vowed never again to work late on his book about destructive cult leaders. In the future, he would write about malignant pied pipers only in early mornings or on weekends.

CPSIA information can be obtained
at www.ICGtesting.com
Printed in the USA
FSHW022302171019
63028FS